ICE

IRON ROGUES MC

FIONA DAVENPORT

ICE

Hayes "Ice" Gallagher found his place with the Iron Rogues after his professional hockey career ended. Just as he was getting ready to settle into his new home, his life got upended again when someone tampered with his motorcycle. But something good came out of the wreck—Ice met Marnie Miller.

The club enforcer wasn't going to let the younger beauty out of his sight until he knew she was safe. And he claimed her as his own.

.

1

ICE

"We'll complete the last of the finishes in the next few days, and then it'll be ready for the final walk-through."

I scanned the space around me, satisfied with how my new house had turned out. "Thanks," I murmured to Don, the owner of the company who'd built two homes for me, including the one a club brother bought from me since he'd needed it more than I did.

The house was big, too big for just me. But when I'd decided to build, I knew I wanted the place where I would hopefully raise my family one day. Not that it was very likely when I hadn't been interested in a woman in more years than I wanted to admit.

Although, I hadn't really made an effort either. During my career as a professional hockey player, I'd solely focused on my job. Then after my injury, I'd put all my energy into recovery.

I'd played the majority of my career for the Tennessee Trojans and had grown to love the state. So when I was forced into retirement, it made sense to put down roots there. Besides, moving back to Michigan, where I'd been raised, had been out of the question. I loved my parents, but they drove my brother and me batshit crazy with their eccentric ways. They were "free spirits" and were very open with...just about everything.

My mother made a lot of her decisions based on the cycles of the moon, and my father believed he was living his third life, having been rejected twice so far. But they had chosen not to force their lifestyle on their kids and hadn't flaunted their beliefs or open relationship, which Nathan and I both appreciated. So we'd had a *relatively* normal childhood, but they'd moved into a "community house" after we left home.

While trying to decide exactly where to settle and what to do with my life—since real estate investment didn't take up much of my time—I connected with a friend I'd grown close with after meeting him my first month with the Trojans.

Wrecker was an officer in the Iron Rogues Motorcycle Club. Since I'd been riding since high school, he'd convinced me to prospect for the club. After so many years of being in a tight circle with my team, I liked the idea of being part of a brotherhood.

The Iron Rogues had given me a purpose. A family. It hadn't taken me long to earn my patch, then to work my way into an enforcer position.

Although I'd enjoyed living the last couple of years in the clubhouse, as several of my brothers had found their old ladies and were starting families, I began to hope I'd find my own woman eventually. And since my other business was real estate, I knew that building a house was a good investment anyway.

However, just as I'd finished, Whiskey had become a parent overnight when his sister died and left his niece in his care. Then he met Ellery, and he needed a place to live immediately. I wasn't in a rush, so I sold him the house and searched for a new place to start over.

Now, the new place was just about done, and while I was happy with the result, it also reminded me that I didn't have anyone to share it with. I mentally sighed, wondering when I'd grown a pussy, and refocused on Don.

"We can walk the grounds now, though," he said as he looked over some papers on a clipboard.

"Sounds good."

We walked through the family room to the glass doors and out to an amazing deck that led down to a sparkling pool. I'd insisted that a child-proof fence surround it, but the wrought-iron structure was open enough to enjoy the view behind the house. It sat on over twenty acres of gorgeous Tennessee land. The area I would live in had been cleared, but otherwise, the plot was mostly wooded and even had a stream running through it.

"This really is a spectacular piece of land," Don commented as we descended the steps of the deck. "I have to say, I was relieved when you managed to convince the owner to sell you the land."

"The judge really made it happen," I explained. "Decided that the zoning could go either way, so he was fine with me choosing to make it residential rather than commercial."

There had been a few bids on the parcel, one of them being a commercial developer intent on turning it into a strip mall. I'd hated the thought of this beautiful, serene land being destroyed to make way for more retail.

And I'd known it would feel like home the second I saw it.

"My foreman mentioned that Keith is still pissed as hell." Don rolled his eyes.

The developer, Keith Franks, was shady as fuck and acted like a petulant child when he didn't get his way. The owner of the space hadn't wanted to sell to him. However, it had been rezoned as commercial recently, so he wasn't positive he could accept my bid. Keith had taken it to a judge, who'd ruled in my favor since one side of the land butted up to the beginning of a residentially zoned area that went on for several miles, while the other side was only twenty minutes from a growing downtown.

I shrugged. "He's being petty. Still trying to get another judge to overturn the ruling."

"You'd think he'd give up now that your house is built."

"He's a cocky son of a bitch who believes money will get him whatever he wants. It's annoying. Doubt he'll take it any further, though. He's not stupid enough to take on the Iron Rogues."

Don nodded, then changed the subject back to the house and pointed out some adjustments they'd made from the notes I'd had the last time we walked the property. He was an honest guy with a stellar reputation. Having seen what he did with the house Whiskey now owned and this new place, I was glad I'd given him the jobs.

"Everything looks great," I told him an hour later as we shook hands on the front step.

"I'll call you when the last details are complete."

I lifted my chin in acknowledgment before turning and heading down the front walkway to the driveway where I'd parked my motorcycle.

My phone rang as I swung my leg over the seat, so I left the engine off and fished my cell out of my pocket. The logo for the New York hockey team, the Navigators, flashed on my screen with my brother's phone number.

"What's up, little brother?" I answered.

"How's the house?" Nathan asked in lieu of a greeting.

"Almost done. It'll be ready when you come to town."

"That's the other reason I called," he informed me. "I need to know how many tickets you want for the game."

My brother and I had both become pro hockey players, but he was still in the sport and played as the starting center for New York. They'd be coming down to Tennessee to play my old team soon, and I definitely wasn't going to miss the game.

"Vince offered me a box," I said with a snicker, referring to the owner of the Tennessee Trojans, who'd remained a friend.

"Fuck that," Nathan snapped. "You don't play for those pansies anymore, and you're gonna be there to root for your brother. I'll make sure you have a box in the Navigators section."

I snorted a laugh. Nobody would ever call my brother gullible or a pushover, but I could always get him riled. And he'd taken the bait.

He sighed. "Why do I always fall for your shit?"

"One of the perks of being the big brother," I teased.

"Bullshit."

"Prove it. Stop being so easy to manipulate."

"You know I'd have gotten you a box if you'd asked," Nathan muttered.

"Yeah," I agreed. "But it's more fun this way."

Nathan grumbled something under his breath, and I laughed again.

We said our goodbyes, and I put my phone back in my pocket, then grabbed the helmet that had been hanging on my handlebars.

A lot of bikers didn't bother with protective gear,

which wasn't the smartest choice in the first place, but it was the lifestyle. However, after playing hockey for the majority of my life, I'd had more than enough broken or shattered bones, torn muscles, and head injuries. So I chose to protect my head from any more trauma.

The engine roared to life, and I flipped up the kickstand before walking the bike back down the driveway. When I reached the road, I took off and left all thoughts behind me as I enjoyed the wind rippling past my body. It was late March, and the weather was growing warm, so the breeze felt good.

Approaching a sharp curve ahead, I eased the brake to slow down. I decelerated for a moment, but then the grip lost its tension, telling me that I no longer had control of the brake. I was just rounding the curve, and with the slight decline of the road, my speed increased and sent my hog careening out of control.

I went flying through the air and landed hard on the ground before I blacked out.

2

MARNIE

I was practically on autopilot as I drove home from the salon where I worked, but when I realized I was behind a motorcycle, I slowed until about eight car lengths were between us. With how tired I was and the sharp curve coming up, I didn't want to get too close to the rider.

That choice turned out to be the right one because I was far enough away to pull over to the side of the road when he lost control of his bike and crashed. I watched in horror as his head hit the road, thankful he was wearing a helmet. He slid a few feet, not moving when his body finally came to a stop.

"Crap, crap, crap," I mumbled, my hands shaking as I put the car in park and pushed the button to kill the engine.

I jumped out of the driver's seat to run over to him, skidding to a stop in the gravel on the side of the road. He was sprawled face down, not moving. Crouching, I noticed the leather vest he was wearing, recognizing the motorcycle club logo on the patch on the back. He was an Iron Rogue.

Under normal circumstances, I'd call 911 right away, but with him being a biker, I wasn't sure what to do. The wives of the president and VP of the Iron Rogues were clients of mine, and the last thing I wanted was to get their husbands jammed up by involving the police. For all I knew, this guy had a gun or something else illegal on him that the cops would find if they came to investigate the accident.

Luckily, I had a way to get ahold of someone who could tell me how to handle this situation. Yanking my cell phone out of my back pocket, I called the salon. Although my shift was over, we were still open for another three hours.

Our receptionist picked up on the second ring. "Chop Chop, how can I help you?"

"Hey, Tori. Could you do me a favor and pull up the alternate number Dahlia Pearson left on her account?" I requested.

"Sure." There was a tapping sound in the background, and then she rattled off the number.

"Thanks."

Taking a deep breath, I punched in the digits she gave me and waited for someone to pick up.

"Iron Rogues," a man growled.

"Um...yeah...I'm not sure who I need to talk to, but one of your guys was just in an accident at the curve on Fisher Street. He's banged up pretty badly," I explained.

"Hold up a second," he barked.

There was the muffled sound of deep voices in the background before another guy came on the line. "This is Wrecker. Who're you?"

"Marnie Miller, sir."

He chuckled. "No need to be formal. I haven't been called sir in a fucking long time, girl. Just tell me what happened and who I'm comin' to help."

After I explained what I saw, I added, "I'm not sure which of your guys he is, though. He's face down on the pavement, and I'm afraid to turn him over. I'm not sure how injured he is."

"Good call. I'll be there with a couple of guys soon. You hold tight," he ordered.

The man groaned and rolled over, and I spotted the patches on the front of his vest. "Wait. He's an enforcer. Ice."

"Ice, shit," he grumbled. "The last thing he needs

is another serious injury. He's barely recovered from the last one."

I glanced down at Ice, wondering what had happened to him. He groaned, his brow furrowing, and I felt a huge surge of relief, almost missing Wrecker's question.

"You call anyone else?"

Although he couldn't see me, I still shook my head. "No. I didn't want to...um..."

"Yeah, another good call. We'll be there soon," he assured before hanging up.

I shoved my phone back in my pocket and stared down at Ice. I almost shrieked when his eyes blinked open. Their pale blue color pierced through me even though they were foggy with confusion, and there was a clear visor between us. "Are you an angel? 'Cause no way did I think I was going to heaven."

The line was corny as heck, but it still got to me. His deep, raspy voice sent a sensual shiver down my spine, which was inappropriate considering the circumstances. Clearing my throat, I murmured, "I guess you can't be as hurt as I thought if you can still flirt."

"I'm used to pain, angel. A little more isn't gonna stop me from hitting on you, no matter how outta practice I am."

He let out a low moan as he reached up to grip his helmet. I wrapped my fingers around his wrist. "I don't think you should take that off. You might have injuries that'll get worse if you move too much."

"Had my bell rung plenty of times and broken more bones than I want to count." He flashed me a cocky grin. "So I know when I'm hurt badly enough to be worried. Don't be afraid, angel. I'm a little banged up, that's all."

Releasing his wrist, I heaved a deep sigh as he removed his helmet. His wince of pain didn't detract from how hot he was, my eyes widening as my gaze swept over his thick, dark hair, full beard, and plump lips. Paired with his icy-blue eyes, it was a lethal combination, even when he wasn't at his best.

And it was more than enough to attract my interest, which was a surprise since I wasn't normally one to gawk at random guys. Or even ones that I knew, really.

"Still okay?" I whispered after he dropped the helmet next to him and slowly sat up.

"Yeah." He raked his fingers through his hair, his gaze darting over my shoulder when the roar of motorcycles reached our ears. "How long was I out? Did you call anyone before I came to?"

"Maybe four or five minutes, tops," I answered.

"I called the clubhouse and talked to a guy named Wrecker. Before that, the receptionist at the salon where I work to get the number."

Some of the tension leaked from his tall, muscular frame. "Good girl."

Holy heck, my inner walls clenched at the compliment. "I do Molly's and Dahlia's hair, so I've heard a few things about the Iron Rogues."

"You do hair?" His gaze raked over me, lingering on my long black locks. "Makes sense. Yours is fucking fantastic."

I bit my bottom lip. "Thanks."

"Never thought I'd be jealous of a prospect, but now I wish I was the one our prez sends out with his old lady," he murmured.

"How come?" I asked, tilting my head to the side.

"'Cause then I woulda met you a fuck of a lot sooner." He gestured to his banged-up body. "And in better condition than this."

My cheeks were still hot when a biker pulled up next to us. Killing his engine, he knocked the kickstand with his boot before climbing off his motorcycle. "Shit, man, you look better than I expected. Blade's on his way to the hospital. Dragged my ass away from my wife and kid thinking you were gonna be near death's door when I got here."

"Tried to control my bike the best I could once I realized I was going down, Whiskey." Ice shrugged. "Not that it did much good. The brakes were shit."

"Fucking hell," Whiskey growled.

"Yup," Ice grunted, shooting a look at me. "But at least I got to be rescued by an angel."

Rolling my eyes, I whispered, "Stop. I didn't do anything except check on you and call your club."

Two more guys pulled up in a truck. Whiskey lifted his chin in greeting as my blush deepened. "Wrecker and Wolf are gonna load your bike up and take it back to the shop."

Both guys climbed out, and the one behind the wheel said, "Drop the gate, Wolf. I wanna grab the bike and get outta here."

"Will do," Wolf muttered as he headed to the back of the truck.

"Ambulance is right behind us," Wrecker warned. "Called for one once I knew we'd beat them here."

"I don't need a fucking ambulance," Ice grumbled.

Wrecker shrugged. "Sorry, man. Blade said to call one. That you needed to be checked out more thoroughly than he could do at the compound's clinic."

"Motorcycle accidents are no joke," Wolf added.

Ice looked as though he was going to argue, but the wail of a siren stopped him from saying anything else. He just reached out to interlace his fingers through mine and waited for the paramedics to exit the ambulance while the guys quietly worked to load his motorcycle into the back of the truck.

Now that the cavalry had arrived—times two—I probably should have left. But something about Ice made me want to stick around. At least long enough to know that he'd be okay.

3

ICE

My angel's hand was engulfed by my much larger one, yet we fit together perfectly. She was small and dainty, and even from our sitting positions, I could tell that she was at least a foot shorter than my six-foot, three-inch height.

Her beautiful, deep green eyes were bright but filled with worry for me, which caused warmth to spread through my chest. One look at her curves had fire sparking in other areas, and my cock swelled, adding to my pain.

Jet-black hair hung in gentle waves down to her belly button. My hands itched to run through the thick, shiny tresses. I wanted to feel its softness and to tug until I pulled her head back, giving me access to her rosy, plush lips and slender throat.

The intense colors of her hair, eyes, and lips accentuated her pale, creamy skin, and I had the urge to lap at it like a cat indulging in a bowl of cream. These thoughts shocked the hell out of me but didn't scare me. Instead, they filled me with certainty. This woman was mine.

My focus on my angel was broken when the paramedics crouched down beside me. She pulled her hand gently, but I refused to let it go. I wasn't ready to be separated from her. Besides, I still needed to find out who she was.

I answered the EMT's questions and let them help me onto a stretcher to take me over to the ambulance.

Honestly, I could have walked and would normally have forced the issue. But I was taking advantage of the concern written all over my girl's face.

"Come with me," I demanded, giving her a pleading expression.

She bit her lip, and my core clenched in anticipation of doing the same thing. "I don't know. My car—"

"One of my brothers will take care of it," I assured her, my grip on her hand forcing her to follow me into the back of the ambulance. Since we were still connected, she sat beside me on the stretcher.

Wrecker appeared at the open doors and gestured toward her vehicle. "Go ahead. We'll take it to—" I shot him a meaningful look, and he broke off abruptly, understanding what I wasn't saying. "We'll make sure it's taken care of."

"Um. Okay," she agreed softly, giving me a sweet smile.

Wrecker lifted his chin at me, and I nodded, knowing he'd gotten the message to take my angel's car back to the compound rather than meet us at the hospital.

One of the paramedics climbed into the back and shut the doors. He glanced at us and frowned. Somehow, I knew he was going to ask my angel to sit in a more secure place, but I still wasn't willing to let her go, so I glared daggers at him. His gaze dropped to my vest, and he swallowed hard, keeping his mouth shut as he took a seat in one of the jump seats. Then he tapped on the divider wall, and the driver pulled onto the road.

"What is your name, angel?" I asked softly.

"Marnie. Um, Marnie Miller."

"Beautiful name for a beautiful woman."

Her cheeks bloomed with pink, and she smiled

adorably. "You're just full of terrible pickup lines, aren't you?"

I grinned and reached out my free hand to brush the pad of one finger over the color on her cheek. "Are they so terrible if they're working?" I teased.

Her blush deepened, and she giggled. "Yes, Ice. They're still terrible."

"Hayes," I muttered.

"Pardon?"

"My name is Hayes," I told her.

"Oh, but your vest says Ice, so I assumed—"

"Ice is my road name," I confirmed. My voice took on a tone of finality when I continued, "But you call me Hayes."

She smiled and cocked her head to the side. "Okay, Hayes."

The sound of my name on her lips shot another bolt of lust straight to my dick.

Giving in to temptation, I used our clasped hands to urge her to scoot up so she was sitting beside my chest rather than my legs. Then I delved my free hand into her hair and ran my fingers through the long, satiny locks. I couldn't wait to feel all that softness brushing against my chest while she rode me. To feel it curled around my hands as I held her head back while I fucked her from behind.

My mind ran wild with images of my fingers plunged into all that inky silk while I guided her head as she swallowed me down her throat. That brought thoughts of my face between her legs, my facial hair leaving whisker burns on the pale skin of her thighs.

Fuck. I needed to get control over myself before I attacked her like a rabid animal.

"So you're a hairdresser?" I grunted, hoping random conversation would help take my mind off all the naughty things I intended to do to her.

"Yes. I work at Chop Chop on Main Street in Old Bridge."

I thought about the little downtown area and remembered seeing a beauty salon. "Near Midnight Rebel?" I clarified.

"Um, yeah. It's just up the block."

I nodded, thinking that I needed to make sure any of the prospects and my brothers who visited our bar should keep an eye on the salon when coming and going.

"What did you mean when you said you were used to pain?"

"I played pro hockey, angel. Pain comes with the territory in that sport."

"You don't anymore?"

I shook my head. "Last time I got injured, it took me out for good."

Relief flashed on her face, and I smirked. "Don't like the idea of me being hurt, angel?" I was glad to see that she was already feeling protective of me since I'd been flooded with possessive instincts the moment I opened my eyes and saw her hovering over me.

Her skin turned pink, but she shook her head. I smiled, happy that she'd been honest rather than trying to be coy about it.

"I'm sorry you had to quit, though."

"I used to be, too," I admitted.

"Used to be?"

Smiling, I played with the ends of her hair while I answered, "From now on, I'll always be grateful that I had to retire."

Marnie tilted her head to the side, studying me curiously. "Why?"

"Because if I hadn't, I never would have met you."

"Oh." Her expression was shy, even as she beamed at me. It was cute as fuck.

"Can, um, can I ask you another question?" she queried softly.

"Anything."

Her whole face flushed, traveling down beneath the collar of her shirt and making me wonder just how far it went. "You said you were out of practice."

I played back our interactions in my head and couldn't figure out what she was talking about. "What?"

"Um, you said something about flirting and being out of practice."

"Ah. Yeah," I acknowledged, remembering my comment from earlier. "That's not a question, though," I teased.

"It's just that...well, I imagine a professional hockey player, especially one as hot as you, has women throwing themselves at you all the time and—"

I placed my finger over her lips as I chuckled. "First of all, I haven't noticed a woman in a long time because I was too busy focusing on my career. Sure, puck bunnies were always around, but they learned quickly that I wasn't someone they'd have any luck with."

Marnie's lips lifted at the corners, and she lost the tension that had crept into her shoulders.

"Second...you think I'm hot?"

She rolled her eyes and giggled. "Like you don't know how sexy women think you are."

Grasping her chin, I looked straight into her eyes when I responded. "I only care about what one woman thinks."

"B-bu-but you just met me," she sputtered.

"Didn't take more than a second to know you were mine, angel."

Before she could reply, the ambulance came to a stop, and the doors flung open.

Blade glanced in, and his brows went up when he saw Marnie sitting beside me and our hands still melded together.

Marnie tried to untangle her fingers from mine and sighed when I refused to let go. "Hayes, I should probably get out of their way."

Blade's lips spread into a grin at her use of my given name. I knew he was gearing up to make a smart-ass comment, so I scowled at him, making him roll his eyes and shrug.

The paramedic who'd ridden with us scooted to the back of the truck and hopped out. Then he held his palm out toward my girl. "Here. I'll help you down."

A growl rumbled in my chest, and Blade quickly nudged the guy away, stepping into his spot. "They need to get you out of the truck," he grumbled at me. Then he reached for Marnie, and I reluctantly let her go. Only because Blade was a happily married man, and I knew he wouldn't be remotely interested in Marnie. Not that it stopped me from grinding my teeth at seeing another man's hands on my angel.

As soon as she was steady on the ground, he released her, causing my irrational anger to recede.

My gurney was removed from the truck, and as they wheeled me past Marnie, I reached out and snatched her hand once more, forcing her to come along.

"Sir—" one of the paramedics began, but he was interrupted by Blade.

"She's fine, Danson. Leave it alone."

No one said another word as they took me to a private room and transferred me onto the bed.

Blade paused just inside the room and withdrew his phone from the pocket of his long white lab coat. "Wolf," he grunted at me as he swiped his finger over the screen. His eyes darted to Marnie as he put the phone to his ear, then he pivoted and strolled out into the hallway.

A nurse took my vitals, and just as she was finishing up, Blade stepped back into the room.

He waited for the staff to leave, assuring them he would make sure I changed into a hospital gown and was given an IV. Then he smiled at my angel. "Marnie, right?"

She nodded with a slight curve to her lips.

"I'm sure you and Ice are probably hungry."

Marnie's stomach chose that moment to growl, and she blushed adorably. "Um, yeah. I didn't eat during my shift and then the accident..."

"Mind running down to the cafeteria and grabbing some food?" Blade asked her.

"Sure."

I wanted to protest, but if Wolf had information about the accident, I wanted to hear it before Marnie found out. And if it was club business, she'd need to be out of earshot anyway.

"Come right back to me," I ordered her gruffly, digging in my pocket to give her some cash.

She gave my hand a gentle squeeze, then let go and walked to the door. My eyes were glued to her swinging hips and curvy ass until she disappeared into the hallway.

"I take it Sheila needs to get working on another vest," Blade drawled as he grabbed a hospital gown from a cupboard near the head of the bed.

"Damn straight," I muttered. My face twisted with disgust when he held out the folded clothing. "I'm fine. Not gonna put on one of those stupid things. Do whatever and let me get back to the clubhouse."

Blade rolled his eyes and shook the garment in front of me. "According to Marnie, you hit your head pretty fucking hard, Ice. You've got scrapes and bruises and a few cuts that need stitches. Not going home until I've treated everything and determined that you don't have a concussion."

"You can do all that shit without making me wear a fucking nightgown. Now, what did Wolf have to say?" I asked, changing the subject.

Blade sighed and tossed the garment on the end of the bed. "Fine. I won't keep you overnight, but your ass is staying in bed tomorrow."

I opened my mouth but shut it when he scowled and pointed a finger at me.

"Or you can stay here tonight *and* tomorrow."

"Asshole," I grumbled.

He shrugged unrepentantly, then walked to a cabinet across the room and opened it, fishing for supplies as he filled me in.

"Brake line was cut."

I frowned. "Wolf did a full maintenance on my bike last week."

"That's what he said. This wasn't an accident. Besides that, the line was sliced just enough that it wouldn't fail at first, which is why you were able to get as far as you did without noticing."

"Shit," I muttered, scrubbing my hand over my face and wincing when my bent arm tugged on some raw skin.

"Fox and Mav are looking into options for anyone who might be targeting you to get to the club, but they don't think that's gonna pan out."

Fox was the club president, and Maverick was our vice president. If this was related to club business, they'd figure it out quicker than anyone else.

"Only other person I can think might be behind this is Keith Franks," I mused, my brow furrowing low. "Assumed he was too much of a pussy to take things this far, but maybe I was wrong."

4

MARNIE

"Sending me to the cafeteria was probably a mistake," I warned as I nudged the door of Hayes's hospital room open with my hip. Luckily, it wasn't latched because I had gone overboard with the snacks. "My sweet tooth took over, and I got three candy bars, a few donuts, two pieces of pie, and a slice of chocolate cake."

Both men turned toward me, humor in their eyes as they took in the heaping tray of food I was carrying. Hayes's lips curved into a grin. "Looks like you wiped them out."

"Yeah, I eat when I'm nervous," I mumbled, setting the tray on the table next to his bed with a shrug.

His smile widened. "If it's because of me, better be the good kind of nervousness."

He was right, but I wasn't going to admit that. Not out loud at least. "Maybe it's from worrying that you're more hurt from the accident than you seem."

"Don't stress about that too much." Hayes jerked his thumb toward the doctor who'd met us in the ambulance bay. "That's what I have him for. Blade will make sure I'm good before he discharges me."

"Blade?" I echoed, glancing at the doctor.

"Yeah," he confirmed with a nod. "When I'm not in scrubs, I wear an Iron Rogues cut, same as this stubborn asshole. That is why he's gonna let me do a thorough examination to make sure he didn't do permanent damage to his thick skull. 'Cause the last thing either of us wants is for our prez to get pissed because I let him walk outta here with a traumatic brain injury or some shit like that."

I narrowed my eyes at Hayes. "Or for me to worry myself sick that you'll fall asleep tonight and never wake up."

"Fine." He heaved a deep sigh. "I'll let Blade run whatever tests are needed."

I beamed a smile at him. "Good."

"But you won't need to worry about me not

waking up because you'll be right next to me," he added with a smirk.

His confidence was a major turn-on, but no matter how much I wanted Hayes, I couldn't agree to spending the night with him when we'd just met. "Don't you think we should go out on at least a few dates before you assume that you'll be able to sweet-talk me into bed? I might not have much experience with guys, but even I've heard of the three-date rule."

Hayes reached out to snag my wrist and tug me toward the side of his bed. Once I was there, he wrapped his arm around my waist and growled, "Don't want to hear about you and other men."

"Then I guess it's a good thing that no experience would've been a more accurate description," I whispered, acutely aware of Blade staring at us. My cheeks filled with heat, and I mentally cursed my fair skin.

"I'm gonna get you in for an MRI before your inner caveman fucks with your head even more than a potential concussion," Blade murmured.

Hayes shook his head and grumbled, "Like you're one to talk."

Blade's deep chuckle trailed after him as he stepped out of the room.

"About you staying with me"—he squeezed my

hand, his ice-blue eyes serious as he looked up at me —"it's not just because I want to get in your pants. Or needing someone to keep an eye on me if it turns out that I have a concussion."

My brows drew together. "It isn't?"

"Wish like hell that the first time I got you in my bed it was just because of the pull between us." His thumb stroked my palm, sending a shock of awareness straight to my core. "But while you were in the cafeteria, I found out that my bike was sabotaged. That means you're a witness to more than just an accident. I don't want anything happening to you, so I'm gonna keep a close eye on you to make sure you're safe."

"I didn't even see much," I protested, shaking my head. "Just you crashing your motorcycle. Nobody hit you or anything like that. I have no idea what's going on. There's no reason for anybody to come after me."

"People do a lotta shit for no good reason," he countered. "No way in hell am I going to let them do it to you."

Just as much as I loved how protective he was being, I hated the idea of someone trying to hurt him. So there was only one answer I could give. "Then I'll come with you."

"Good," he grunted.

I wagged my finger at him. "But we'll need to stop at my apartment first to grab some stuff. I can be pretty high maintenance, especially when I'm going into the salon. Clients expect me to look my best if they're going to trust me with their hair."

His gaze drifted over my long black locks. "If that's how women pick their hairdresser, you gotta have a fuck ton of clients because your hair is fucking fantastic."

Butterflies swirled in my belly. I'd had plenty of people compliment me on my hair, but it meant more coming from Hayes. "Thanks."

I waited in his room while hospital staff came and went, taking him for the tests Blade wanted to run. It took a few hours, so it was good I'd grabbed so many snacks from the cafeteria because we went through them all. When he was discharged, I instinctively reached for my purse and remembered it wasn't there. "Darn it. I hope whoever drove my car here locked it and my bag is still inside. Canceling my cards and replacing my driver's license is a headache I don't want to deal with."

"Your purse will definitely still be there," he assured me.

I tilted my head to the side. "You seem very certain of that."

"Yeah, because your car is in the safest place in town—the Iron Rogues compound."

My eyes widened. "It is?"

"Yup."

I laughed softly. "I guess you were pretty darn confident that I was leaving here with you."

He nodded. "Damn straight."

I narrowed my eyes. "Even before you knew about your bike being messed with."

"Like I said, I have more than one reason for wanting you to spend tonight with me."

He wasn't even a tiny bit embarrassed to have been caught, which somehow didn't surprise me. "Hopefully, you also have a plan for how we're getting out of here since your bike was hauled away from the accident and my car is at the compound."

"Sure do," he confirmed with a grin as he shrugged on his leather vest. "One of our prospects will meet us outside."

Blade poked his head into the room. "Now that I know you didn't do irreparable damage to your thick skull, I'm headed back home."

Hayes flashed him a smile. "Thanks for coming in to make sure I'm good."

"No thanks necessary, Ice." Blade shrugged off his gratitude. "Just part of my duties as the club's doctor."

"Sure does come in handy," I murmured as Hayes stood and settled his palm against my lower back to guide me out of the room.

"Like you wouldn't believe," Hayes muttered.

I wasn't sure that I wanted to know what he meant by that, so I didn't ask any questions as he led me outside. An SUV idled at the curb, and a guy jumped out of the driver's seat to open the back door. "Hey, Ice. Glad to see that you're okay."

"Thanks." Hayes jerked his chin in recognition before helping me into the back seat and climbing in after me.

When the prospect pulled away from the curb, I leaned forward to give him my address. It wasn't long before we pulled through the gate at my complex, and he waited in the vehicle while Hayes came upstairs with me.

I grabbed a weekender tote bag big enough for a couple of days' worth of stuff, but he shook his head. "You're gonna need more than that."

"I am?" I asked, my brows drawing together.

"You're high maintenance, remember?" he teased.

I rolled my eyes. "Yeah, but I don't need a ton of stuff for one night."

"Sorry, angel." He reached up to grab my rolling carry-on from the shelf in my closet. "Not sure how long it's gonna take to clear up this mess, but I'm not gonna let you outta my sight until I do."

Considering I barely knew Hayes, I probably should have asked more questions. But something told me I could trust him. So I packed a week's worth of clothes and all of my favorite toiletries into two bags.

I stuck my tongue out at him when he teased, "Damn, I shoulda had the prospect come up with us to help with the bags."

"I warned you," I murmured as I rolled the smaller of the two out the door with his laughter trailing me.

5

ICE

The SUV rolled to a stop in front of the clubhouse, and the prospect who was driving hopped out. Marnie was curled into my side but sprang upward and scooted over when the door beside her opened as if she'd been caught making out in the back seat. Which had definitely crossed my mind, but I wasn't gonna risk anyone hearing her sounds of pleasure. And I wasn't sure I'd be able to stop once I had my mouth on her.

I almost growled at the prospect to keep his hands off my woman, but as much as I hated to admit it, my body was weak from the accident. Clenching my jaw, I allowed the little shit to help Marnie out of the SUV while I carefully exited the other side. Slowly, I walked to the front of the vehicle, where she waited for me. Taking her hand, I led her up to the front door and into the clubhouse.

The prospect followed, carrying her shit, and I quietly instructed him to take it to my room.

"Marnie!"

Molly, our VP's old lady, drew my attention as she rushed across the lounge and pulled Marnie in for a hug. As she drew back, she glanced down at the hand I'd refused to let go of and chuckled.

I drew Marnie close and released her, only to drop my arm over her shoulders, barely holding back a wince when it stretched my stiff muscles.

Blade's wife, Elise, walked over to join us, greeting Marnie with a happy, familiar smile. "It's great to see you!" Her eyes shifted to my arm, and her smile turned mischievous. "I take it you'll be staying a while? At least until Ice's house is finished? We can finally have that lunch we are always talking about."

I frowned at Elise, warning her not to take her teasing too far. Marnie and I hadn't gone into depth about how long she'd be staying with me. Or about moving into my place.

Marnie tipped her head back to look up at me. "A house?"

"We'll talk about it later, angel," I murmured before kissing her temple.

Fox, the Iron Rogues prez, walked into the room holding one of his six-week-old twins. He held the door open, and his old lady, Dahlia, followed him, carrying the other baby.

"Hey, Marnie," Dahlia greeted her warmly. She walked up to my angel and gave her a one-armed hug. "I'm glad to see you. I wanted to thank you for calling the clubhouse when you found Ice."

Marnie shrugged, and her cheeks turned pink. "After everything you'd told me about your husband and the Iron Rogues, I figured you guys would want to know first."

I tucked her in a little closer to my side and kissed the top of her head. "You did great, angel."

"Um...who's this little doll?" Marnie queried, changing the subject.

I loved how Marnie blushed when praised, but I was gonna have to get my girl used to taking compliments.

"This is Violet," Dahlia replied with a soft expression as she stared down at her daughter. "Kye is holding her twin, Jett."

"They are absolutely adorable," Marnie gushed.

Dahlia held Violet out a little and offered, "Would you like to hold her?"

"Yes!" Marnie bounced on her toes happily before reaching out to carefully transfer the baby into her arms, forcing me to reluctantly let her go.

My mouth curled up as I observed my angel with a little one cuddled in her embrace. I couldn't wait to see her holding our baby. An image of Marnie round with my baby made my dick harden. If I had my way—and I was fucking determined to get it—she'd be knocked up sooner rather than later.

"Baby," Fox murmured as he came to stand next to his wife. "Need to talk to Ice for a minute, can you take Jett?"

After he'd handed over his son, he looked at me and jerked his head toward the hallway that led to his office.

I jerked my chin up in acknowledgment, then turned to Marnie. "You hungry, angel?"

"Yup," she confirmed with a distracted nod as she stared down at Fox's daughter. "I've only had hospital snacks since the start of my shift today."

"We'll take her to the kitchen for some food," Molly volunteered.

I nodded my thanks, then planted a quick kiss on

Marnie's lips, chuckling at her stunned expression. "Be right back," I told her before striding away.

When I walked into Fox's office, Maverick lounged on a sofa in a seating area off to the side of the room.

"Tell me about the situation with the developer," Fox demanded. "Mav and I haven't come up with any club-related issues that would warrant someone sabotaging your bike."

Sitting in the chair in front of his desk, I gave them a rundown on Keith Franks and his bullshit. "Having a hard time seeing that little shit as someone with the balls to fuck with an Iron Rogue. He's also a fucking idiot, though, so maybe he felt safe with his plan since there were no witnesses. My security cameras aren't online yet."

Mav chuckled, and I twisted my head to look his way.

"No witnesses, huh?"

My head cocked to the side, and I answered, "Yeah."

"Take it you didn't clarify that with the woman you showed up with?"

I narrowed my eyes and pierced him with an icy stare. "Your point?"

"You know we don't allow puck or club bunnies

here, so I'm assuming you found your woman." Mav grinned widely. "Coulda sworn you said you've never be pussy-whipped like us."

I wanted to deny it, but he wasn't wrong. As much as I'd longed for a family, I never expected to be knocked on my ass by an angel and find myself completely obsessed with her. I'd only known Marnie for a few hours, but I knew I'd do anything to keep her and make her happy.

"Guess I was wrong," I admitted since I had no defense. "I'll be talking with Sheila tomorrow."

She was the old lady of one of our older members, Tank. In the past, we'd ordered our cuts and property vests, only using Sheila's sewing skills in an emergency. But after Mav and Fox fell hard and fast for their women, they'd wanted their mark on them as fast as possible—something I now understood.

Fox had followed the example of Mac, his father-in-law and the president of the Silver Saints MC. They'd been in the same position, with the patches in a rush to get a vest on their women. So Mac had taken to keeping a stash of cuts that had the property embroidery finished and only needed the names added. Which Sheila happily offered to do for us when our prez stocked up.

Mav laughed and crossed his arms over his chest. "Molly texted Sheila as soon as she heard you were bringing a woman here."

I double blinked, confused. "How did she—never mind." The realization hit me, and I rolled my eyes. "You assholes gossip like little old ladies."

Fox cleared his throat, drawing our attention back to him. "Let's get this shit done. Want to get back to my wife and kids." His gaze swept over me, and he grimaced. "Besides, you look like shit, and I know Blade ordered you to rest if he was gonna let you out of the hospital."

"Gossips," I grumbled, annoyed that Blade had told the prez, knowing Fox would demand I do as the doctor said. And I didn't want to admit that I was exhausted and in a fuck ton of pain.

"Back to the accident..."

We spent the next twenty minutes going over everything I knew about Keith and what options we had in dealing with the shady fucker.

"Now you look like death warmed over," Maverick muttered with a frown.

"Flattery will get you nowhere with me, brother," I deadpanned, making both men chuckle.

"Get your ass to bed, Ice," Fox ordered. "Gonna need you when we go after this son of a bitch."

Too tired to argue, I nodded and stood. Then I made my way toward the kitchen, intent on finding my girl and going to bed as I'd been instructed to do.

A couple of other old ladies had joined the party, and the women were all gathered around one of the large tables in the spacious kitchen. A lot of the members lived in the clubhouse, but even the single guys who had places off the compound often showed up for meals. So there was plenty of room to accommodate a good-sized crowd of people.

The girls were giggling, and a smile tugged at my lips when I heard the sweet sound of Marnie's laughter. I liked seeing her so at ease with the other old ladies. She'd mentioned doing Molly's and Dahlia's hair, but I hadn't realized they were also friends. And it seemed she'd met Elise recently and would be taking her on as a client as well.

She would fit right in with the whole group, and I was glad for it...since she would be one of them soon.

"Angel," I murmured as I stopped beside her. "Have you eaten enough?"

"I'm full," she replied with a smile.

Fuck, I wish that was true. I wanted her stuffed full of me. "Let's get you settled, then I need to get some rest."

"Your doctor is being a hard-ass, huh?" Elise teased.

"Don't answer that."

I glanced at the back door and saw our club doctor striding toward us, scowling. "If you mention my wife and ass in the same sentence, I'll put you back in the hospital."

Rolling my eyes, I cupped Marnie's elbow. "Ready?"

"Good night, ladies," she chirped, then let me help her up and waved as we walked away.

The second and third floors of the clubhouse were almost all rooms for the members. Some who lived here—all the time or part time—and others set aside for guests.

When we reached the second floor, I walked past the first two doors, which happened to be empty rooms, and stopped in front of my own. Then I fished out a key from my pocket, unlocked the door, and gestured for Marnie to enter ahead of me.

I was never more grateful for my innate neatness because the room was picked up and clean. The space was simple, with a king-sized bed, a long dresser across from it, and a massive flat screen mounted on the wall. The only other furniture was a standing lamp, small chair, and side table in the corner.

"There's a bathroom through that door," I told her, pointing to the right. "And a closet there." I pointed at a door on the left. "There are a few empty drawers in the dresser, or you can hang whatever you want in the closet."

Marnie looked around curiously and cocked an eyebrow when her gaze landed on my face. "You live here?"

"Yeah." My brow furrowed as I scanned the space, wondering what was wrong with it.

"I just...um, there's nothing personal here. It feels like a hotel room."

I chuckled and set her bag on top of the dresser before moseying over to her. "Most of my shit is packed in boxes since I'll be moving into my house soon."

It took a monumental effort not to refer to it as *our* house.

"Your house...right." She looked a little sad, and I wasn't sure why. I just knew I didn't like it.

"We can talk about that another time, angel. Right now, I need to thank you."

"Thank me?" The genuine confusion in her expression was adorable. She was so sweet and innocent, it probably made me a bastard that I intended to corrupt my pretty little angel. Not that it made a difference. Nothing was gonna stop me from making Marnie mine.

"You stopped to help me when a lot of people would have just driven right by. Then were smart enough to call my brothers instead of the police. And you've stayed by my side since the accident. So I'm incredibly grateful."

I cupped her cheeks and held her head steady while I lowered my mouth to hers. When our lips touched, she gasped, and I took advantage of the opportunity to gently slip my tongue inside her mouth, giving her time to get used to me.

It had only taken me a second to recognize that she didn't have any experience with kissing. And damn, it made me hard as fuck to think that I was going to be the one to teach her.

It also told me that she was most likely a virgin. My cock throbbed, loving the idea of being the first and only dick to sink into her tight pussy.

Tentatively, the tip of her tongue touched mine, and I groaned, turned the fuck on by her desire. Slanting my head, I moved my hands to her neck and used my thumbs to tilt her chin up, giving me better access.

After a few minutes of devouring her delectable mouth, I felt my body reaching the point of no return. It was oh-so tempting to lay her down on the bed and take her cherry, but I was still sore and tired from my accident. She deserved the best for her first time, and I wouldn't be able to give her that tonight.

Besides, it was probably a smart idea to give her a little time to get to know me before we fucked. We were already going to be moving at warp speed in this relationship, and I didn't want to scare her into running.

With a deep groan, I ripped my mouth away and rested my forehead against hers. The only sound in the room was our panting breaths, but I could have sworn I heard our racing heartbeats.

After a minute or two, I felt more in control of my body and managed to step back. "Go get ready for bed, angel," I told her in a gritty voice. My hands went to her shoulders, and I turned her around, then patted her curvy ass before urging her toward the bathroom.

Rather than digging in her bag for her pajamas, I stalked to my dresser and pulled out one of my T-shirts. It would dwarf her small body, but if I couldn't have her in my bed naked, then she was damn well gonna be wearing my clothes.

When she stepped back into the room, I was already in bed, attempting to read. I'd been sucked into the thriller when I first started it, but my thoughts kept straying to my angel tonight, so I'd read the same paragraph five times.

"You wear glasses?" Marnie asked, her cheeks dusting with pink.

"Only for reading. Do they bother you?" I doubted it, if her blush was anything to go by.

"No...um...it's just, I guess I never expected to see someone like you wearing them." She giggled and climbed onto the bed, then pointed at the tattoo that covered one of my arms from shoulder to wrist. "It's just a little funny to see a big, bad, tattooed biker looking a little nerdy."

"Nerdy?" I growled playfully.

She dropped her gaze to the comforter as she pushed it back and slipped under it before yanking the material back up to her waist. "Um...yeah. But you know, in a really sexy way."

I grinned and shook my head as I set my book on the nightstand next to me.

"Come here," I murmured, holding my arm open. She didn't hesitate to scoot over and cuddle into my side. "As hot as it makes me to hear you say you think I'm sexy, we both need our rest."

Sighing, I kept her plastered to my body as I maneuvered us to lie down. I kissed the top of her head, then rested my cheek on her crown while my fingers toyed with her gorgeous hair. "Night, angel."

She made a little humming sound and snuggled closer, making my dick jump in an attempt to get to her. I silently cursed, expecting to be up half the night with blue balls. However, the accident and very long day caught up to me, and it only took a few moments for me to pass out.

6

MARNIE

It took my brain a moment to click on when my eyes blinked open the next morning, but once it did, my lips curved into a huge grin. With Hayes wrapped around me, his arm flung over my waist and his thick thigh wedged between my legs, it was a great way to wake up. One I hoped to experience again and again.

When I saw Hayes crash his motorcycle, I had no idea it was going to change my life. But even though the past day had been full of surprises—and had put me in enough danger that Hayes insisted I stay at the clubhouse—I had no regrets over stopping to help him. Not only was it the right thing to do...it also landed me in bed with the sexy biker who'd brought my dormant libido roaring to life.

"Morning," Hayes rasped, his arms tightening around me. "Sleep good?"

I nodded, cuddling my back deeper against his chest. "Yeah, better than I expected since I'm not used to having anyone else in bed with me."

"You better not be," he growled, brushing his lips against the top of my head. "But that's gonna change now that you have me."

"I like the sound of that," I admitted softly.

"Fuck, angel," he groaned. "I hate to be the one to say it, but we better get moving if we're going to make it to the salon on time."

"Wait a second." Twisting around, I blinked up at him. "You were serious about that?"

"As a heart attack," he confirmed with a nod, his blue eyes gleaming with determination. "Nobody is gonna hurt you on my watch."

When he said stuff like that, it was difficult to remember that I was supposed to go into the salon instead of just convincing him we should spend the day in bed together. "But don't you have other stuff you need to do? It's going to be a long one since I need to be there from eight until five, with back-to-back appointments all day except for my lunch break."

"I got nothing on my calendar that's more important than you." He winked and slid out of bed, holding his hand out to me. "Knew that dumping my hockey money into real estate was a good call, but now I have another reason to be grateful for it— plenty of free time to watch over you."

"Okay, but you're going to be bored," I warned as I climbed off the mattress with his help.

He shook his head with a sexy smirk. "Not a chance in hell when I get to watch you all day."

I found his confidence amusing because there was no chance he'd be happy sitting in an uncomfortable chair surrounded by gossiping women. But I wasn't going to argue with him when I enjoyed having him around. Spending my workday with Hayes nearby wasn't going to be a hardship for me like it was for him.

"Alrighty then." I gestured toward the en suite bathroom. "You're probably going to want to get ready first because it will take me a while to do my hair and makeup after my shower."

His eyes heated as his gaze swept down the T-shirt he'd given me to wear to bed last night. "If I didn't know damn well that it'd end up taking us a fuck of a lot longer, I'd say we should shower together. But there's no chance I'd be able to keep my hands off your naked, wet body. Or my tongue."

While my core clenched in response to the dirty picture he painted with his words, I gasped. Taking advantage of my parted lips, Hayes lowered his head to capture my mouth in a deep kiss that left me breathless. I didn't come out of my sensual stupor until I heard the shower come on after he padded into the bathroom.

"Whoa," I panted, using my hand to fan my face before I went into the closet to grab some clothes and my hair dryer.

Hayes got ready as quickly as I expected, and I took as long as I warned him. But he put that time to good use by getting me a travel mug of coffee and a bagel with cream cheese to enjoy while he drove my car to the salon.

"Thanks so much," I mumbled around the last bite of bagel as we pulled into the lot behind the salon.

"It was my pleasure, angel." He turned toward me after killing the engine. "I like making sure you have what you need."

I squirmed in my seat. "You can't say stuff like that when I only have a couple of minutes before I need to clock into work."

"How come?"

"Because you're too darn sexy for my own good."

Feeling more daring than I ever had before, I added, "And it makes me want to climb you like a monkey."

"Shit, angel." He reached down to adjust the hard length pressing against his zipper. "Now I'm gonna need a minute before I walk in there, or else I'm gonna scare all the customers away."

Knowing I had that effect on him sent a feminine thrill through me, and there was a little extra sway to my hips as he followed me into the salon. After he swept his gaze over the space, he settled himself in the waiting area, choosing a spot where he could see me the whole time.

Before heading over to my station, I leaned close and whispered, "I will totally understand if you get bored and want to bail. I'll be safe, surrounded by plenty of people all day."

"Not gonna happen, angel," he assured.

Hayes ended up proving me wrong about being happy while he hung around. Seven hours and six clients later, he was kicked back in the salon owner's chair—which Peggy had happily rolled out of her office first thing this morning so he didn't have to squish into one of the seats in the waiting area. Her idea, not mine. Even though she never let anyone so much as touch that chair because she loved it so much.

And that wasn't the last time someone at the salon surprised me. I had expected my coworkers to be uneasy with having a guy invade our space, but they'd barely blinked when Hayes announced that he was staying to keep an eye on me. The single ones had done a lot of fluttering of their lashes at him, though. Which hadn't made me happy at all.

But my current customer took it further than that. If Candi didn't stop soon, she would find herself with a nasty surprise when she looked in the mirror after I finished her hair. If she could even manage to look past her boobs with how they were almost spilling out of the top she kept pulling down.

"Here," I grunted, shoving a black cape at her. "You better put this on so you don't get any stray pieces on your shirt."

"Uh, okay. I guess." She made a big show of putting it on, lifting her arms high enough that the bottom of her bra showed while she stared at Hayes. When he didn't react, her shoulders slumped, and she dropped onto the chair, where I used a little too much force to whirl her around so she wasn't facing him anymore.

Feeling jealous was a new experience for me, and I didn't like it one bit. I knew I wasn't being reasonable since Hayes had barely glanced at any of the women who'd tried hitting on him today, but that didn't soothe the green-eyed monster inside me that wanted to hack their hair off instead of styling it how they asked.

It didn't help that I kept wondering what would happen when Hayes moved into his house. Would he want me to stay at the clubhouse for my safety? Or was he thinking about taking me with him?

The questions rattling around inside my head drove me up the wall. The day couldn't end fast enough for me, and it had nothing to do with how much my feet ached.

7

ICE

M arnie collapsed onto the bed with a deep sigh.

"My feet are killing me," she groaned.

I hated that she was in pain, but it had been clear that she loved her job and clients. So instead of convincing her to quit, I removed her boots and socks before digging my thumbs into the arches.

"Oh, that feels good," she moaned.

Fucking hell. I was gonna explode before I ever got inside her if she didn't stop saying shit like that in her sexy, breathy voice.

"I aim to please," I teased as I dropped to my knees in front of her. My hands worked upward toward her toes, and my cock continued to grow harder as more little moans escaped her plush, pink lips.

Marnie's eyes fluttered closed as she lay sprawled over the mattress. "Mmm, Hayes, you're so good at that."

My voice was raspy when I responded. "Angel, you can't say shit like that right now, or I'm gonna lose my mind."

Her eyes flew open, and she stared at my face, a pretty blush spreading down and disappearing into her shirt.

Sliding my hands up, I massaged her ankles and then her calves, continuing until I was between her thighs.

I drew one finger up her center, and she gasped, her eyes widening.

"You like that, angel?" I asked, cupping her pussy over her black pants. Her heat seared my flesh even through the dense material.

"Yes," she whispered, leaning up on her elbows to see me better.

I traced the seam of her pants with a finger again and licked my lips when a wet spot began to appear. "Has anyone ever touched you like this before?"

She swallowed hard, shaking her head so her long black hair swished around her shoulders.

"No. No one has ever...um...I've never..." Her cheeks heated, and she glanced away, looking embarrassed. "No one's ever been, um, down there."

A guttural groan escaped my chest as I reached up and grasped her chin, forcing her to look at me. "I'm gonna be the first one to ever get between these sexy thighs, angel?"

"Uh-huh." She must have seen how fucking hot that made me because some of the embarrassment in her expression began to fade.

She'd already admitted to being a virgin but hearing her confirm that I was the only man who'd ever been—and ever would be—between her legs made me want to rip off her clothes and sink my naked cock into her tight, untouched pussy. But knowing that this would be painful for her gave me the strength to give her one chance to back out.

If she needed a little more time to get used to the idea, I didn't know how, but I would give it to her. This *would* be happening, but I could be patient. *Probably.* "Do you want me to stop?"

I ground the heel of my hand into her center, and she gasped, "No."

Before I knew what was happening, she jack-knifed off the mattress and gripped the side of my cut, pulling me to her so she could crush her lips against mine.

Damn, she was so fucking perfect. Even if she hadn't been a virgin, I wouldn't have wanted her any less, but being the only man to sink inside her, to feel her heat wrapped around their cock, to know what she looked and sounded like when she came...it pushed me near my breaking point. I wanted to shove my cock deep inside her and fuck her hard and fast, but I knew I needed to take my time if I wanted to avoid hurting her too much.

So even though the woman was fucking killing me with her sweet little moans and the promise of her hot, naked body writhing beneath me, I reached deep down and clung to my control.

My hand moved between her thighs again, and she scooted forward, circling her legs around my torso and grinding her hips to increase the friction.

"Greedy little thing, aren't you, angel?" I asked against her lips.

She pulled her head back at my question, and I could see the hesitancy in her gaze.

"I love that you want me so much, baby," I growled. "I want you desperate for me. Begging for the pleasure only I will ever give you."

I rubbed harder and faster, focusing on the spot right over her clit.

"Oh, Hayes," she cried out. "Yes!"

My cock throbbed in sync with my racing pulse and come oozed from the tip.

I pushed gently against her shoulder, urging her to lay back on the bed once more. Then I leaned over her and took her lips in a devouring kiss. Our tongues tangled, gliding against each other in a sensual dance that fanned the flames inside me.

"I want you," she whispered against my lips.

Dammit all to hell. How was I supposed to resist her when she said shit like that?

"It's your first time, angel," I groaned. "I need to get you ready."

After placing a quick kiss on her lips, I trailed my lips down her neck. I didn't stop until I reached the hint of cleavage peeking out from the top of her blouse.

Slowly, I popped each button down the center, my eyes eager to find out how far the pink flush spreading over her skin went. When the last button was released, I pushed the sides of her shirt away, and fire licked at my insides as I stared at the color disappearing into her jeans.

I was gonna taste every inch of her delicious curves, starting with her big sexy tits.

"Up," I instructed.

She immediately raised her torso so I could help her sit. Then I pushed her shirt off her shoulder and deftly popped the catch on the back of her bra. When it fell, baring her luscious mounds, I sucked in a breath.

"Fucking beautiful," I rasped. "Scoot up the bed, angel."

She moved into position, and I climbed on, hovering over her as my eyes drank in the beauty in front of me. I plunged one of my hands into her incredible hair, letting it sift through my fingers before I used it to pull her head up so I could take her mouth again.

Once I finished ravishing her lips, I bent down and swirled my tongue around each pretty pink nipple.

Marnie moaned, arching her back to get her tits closer to my mouth.

I chuckled around a mouthful of her breast. "Such a greedy angel. It's hot as fuck."

After loving on her tits until she was breathless and squirming with desire, I kissed down her chest, stopping to circle her belly button with my tongue. Then I flicked open the snap, hooked my fingers into her waistband, and dragged her pants and lace panties down her legs.

Her bare pussy was dripping wet, begging for my tongue to lap up all that glistening arousal.

Settling between her legs once more, I ran my thumb down her drenched center, loving the way she shivered under my touch.

"Do you know how perfect you are, angel?"

She didn't answer, her eyelids fluttering closed.

"Eyes, angel. You're going to watch me eat this beautiful pussy."

She quickly opened them, the green pools widening as she watched me bend over her sex.

I slowly licked up her slit, humming apprecia-tively at the taste of her sweetness.

"Mmm, you're so sweet."

Sliding a finger inside her tight channel, I swirled it around. Her legs shook, and she arched her back, causing the digit to sink in even farther. But just before she fell over the edge, I pulled out.

She whimpered, her bright green orbs pleading for release.

"Taste yourself, angel."

Putting my fingers to her lips, she touched them

with just the tip of her tongue. I pressed them between her lips, and it seemed to be the ticket to her confidence because she grabbed my wrist and licked the digits clean. Her eyes stayed glued to mine the entire time, making my skin prickle with energy.

Fuck. I was already hard as steel, but now my cock was pressing painfully against my zipper, the grooves digging into the sensitive flesh. He wanted out. Wanted to be buried inside our angel's tight grip and scorching heat.

But I wasn't going to let him out until Marnie came on my tongue.

"That's so fucking hot, angel," I murmured, pulling my fingers from mouth and tracing her lips before trailing the tips down between her tits, all the way back to her dropping center.

Sliding a digit inside again, I groaned. She was so fucking tight, and I wasn't a small man. I needed to stretch her for my cock, so I added another finger, swirling them before adding a third. Moving them in and out, I sucked her hardened clit in the same rhythm.

Marnie's hips bucked, her body eager to meet my mouth. With a passionate cry, her orgasm crashed into her, and she came hard and fast.

I growled, lapping up all of her juices as they

gushed into my mouth. When I was satisfied with my meal, I crawled over her and dropped my head to kiss her, letting her taste herself on my lips.

She was panting heavily when I pulled back, but her pretty mouth formed a cute little pout. "Seems a little unfair that I'm the only one not wearing any clothes."

Staring down into her beautiful eyes, I smirked. "You want me naked, angel?"

"Yes, please," she said shyly as her warm hands slid under the front of my shirt.

It amazed me that even after letting go of her inhibitions and coming in my mouth, she was still so innocent. It fueled the possessiveness inside me, making me even more determined to always protect and care for her. Marnie was mine, and it was time to prove it to both of us.

I quickly divested myself of my clothing, then knelt between her spread legs.

Her eyes trailed down my arms, and I was happy to see her eyes darkening with desire as they lingered on my tattoos. She licked her lips when her perusal moved to my chest and down to my stomach before zeroing in on my big, hard cock.

Her eyes widened, and her mouth formed a little O.

"It will fit, angel," I assured her.

She looked dubious and curious at the same time. After a few seconds, she reached down and wrapped one of her hands around my cock—though she was only able to get about halfway around because her hands were small and my shaft was long and thick.

I groaned when she squeezed and glided her hand up to the angry purple head, spreading the precome around with her thumb.

"Fuck, baby," I grunted, grabbing ahold of her wrist and reluctantly removing it from my dick. "I'm already worked up enough, but when I come, it's gonna be in your tight little pussy."

Marnie dropped her hand to the bed beside her and stared at me through hooded eyes. She bit her lip nervously, then took a deep breath and spread her thighs even wider, her soaked pussy dripping and waiting for me.

"You're gonna be tight as fuck because it's your first time. I'll take it slow, and you tell me if it hurts," I whispered, running the head of my cock against her swollen clit.

"Please, Hayes," she whimpered.

"Don't worry, angel. You'll get what you want. Gonna take this sweet cherry you saved for me."

Inch by inch, I sunk my cock into her slippery

channel, pausing when I bumped against her virginity. Grimacing because I knew there was no way to avoid the pain, I plunged right through her barrier, fully seating myself in one thrust. I hoped getting it over with so swiftly would ease the sting a little quicker.

She sucked in a deep breath, making her tits bounce and her pussy clamp tight around my cock. I squeezed my eyes closed and thought of anything that would decrease my need so I didn't lose my shit and fuck her into oblivion before she was ready.

"Okay, angel?" I gritted out, my jaw clenched so hard my teeth ached.

"Yes," she murmured tentatively. "The pain is almost gone."

I shifted my position, and she moaned, her expression blissful. "How does that feel?"

"Good," she murmured. "So full."

Slowly, I pulled nearly all the way out, then slid back in, gliding along her walls while my hands caressed her tits.

"More," she begged softly.

"Fuck," I grunted, increasing my speed little by little, and punched my hips just a bit harder.

With every little moan that fell from her plush

lips, my balls swelled until they were painfully tight. The need to claim her slammed into me with each thrust. I needed to make her mine. To fill her womb with my come until there was no doubt I'd left a part of me behind. It was unlikely that my little virgin was on birth control, and I hadn't even considered fucking her with protection.

But I wasn't going to come until I gave her another climax. It would help stretch her even more and soften her cervix so she took in all my seed.

Sliding my hand between us, I rubbed her swollen clit as I pounded my cock in and out of her.

"Oh, Hayes," she moaned, wrapping her legs around me and pumping her hips to meet every thrust. "Yes! Right there! Oh, yes!"

Her whole body shook as her orgasm approached the peak, then she screamed my name as she flew apart, and her pussy drenched my cock.

"Fuck!" I shouted. Feeling her ultimate arousal flooding her channel, making her slick so I easily glided in and out shattered my control. I slammed home one last time, filling her with every inch of me before I exploded.

Hot jets of semen spurted from my cock over and over as my body vibrated with the force of my climax. I rocked against Marnie and was pleased when she tensed, her breaths escalating again.

Fuck yeah. If she came while I was shooting my load inside her, there was an even better chance that I'd knock her up.

My cock had barely softened, so I quickly built up speed again and pinched her hard little clit, sending her careening into oblivion once more. To my shock, I was wracked with another orgasm and released more come.

When the shudders subsided and my pulse began to slow, I collapsed onto her, though I was careful not to crush her since she was so tiny compared to me. I laid my head on her chest, and the fingers of one hand absently played with her hair.

After a few minutes, I leaned up and kissed each of her pretty pink nipples before dragging my lips down her stomach, where I lingered for just a moment. Then I shuffled my position so I was lying between her legs, my face hovering just above her pussy.

"How are you feeling, angel?" I inquired as I used my thumbs to part her folds. She was a little red and raw, which kept me from taking her again when I spied the tinge of pink in her juices. It was fucking hot to see the proof that she was, and would only ever be, mine.

I mentally lectured myself to get my head right. Marnie needed a bath and rest, not another hard fuck.

She sighed. "Amazing."

I chuckled at the dreamy expression on her face as I slid back up her body. Stopping at her stomach, I kissed it, hoping it would soon be round with my baby. But if it hadn't happened this time, I'd keep trying until it did.

Continuing, I left a trail of kisses on her silky skin until we were face-to-face. She smiled sweetly, her sleepy eyes drooping, and my lips curled up before I pressed my mouth to hers. "Come on, angel. I need to clean you up and get you into a bath, or you're gonna be sore as fuck tomorrow. Then you can sleep."

She grumbled as I climbed off the bed and scooped her into my arms. Then she laid her head on my shoulder, and her arms locked around my neck.

"Are you going to take a bath with me?" she asked before rubbing her lips on my neck.

"Tempting, angel. You have no idea how tempting. But if I get in the tub with your sexy, wet, naked body, I won't be able to control myself."

She raised her head, and a cute little pout pursed her lips.

I chuckled and gave her a quick kiss.

"But I'll hold you all night."

She seemed satisfied with my answer, laying her head back on my shoulder with a contented sigh.

8

MARNIE

All that worrying I'd done about Hayes leaving me at the compound when he moved into his house had been for nothing. Only one week later, not only was it fully furnished with brand new furniture that he'd asked me to pick out during my days off, but just about all of my clothes and toiletries were in the primary closet and bathroom.

The day after he did the final walk-through with the builder, we'd stopped at my apartment to pick up what I thought would only be a few more things. Instead, he'd had a prospect follow us in an SUV... with four extra suitcases. Big ones, too.

I wasn't sure how many trips it would take me to get all my things back to my apartment after this was all over. But with how Hayes kept calling the house our home, I was hoping I'd never have to find out.

We hadn't really put a label on our relationship yet, but I was meeting his brother today. Which had to mean something. Or at least that was what I kept telling myself.

"You're sure Nathan doesn't want to stay here instead?" I asked for the fifth time, worried that I'd scared off his younger brother.

"I'm positive, angel." Hayes brushed his lips against mine and murmured, "He's got his own room at the hotel. He'll be fine."

"Okay," I sighed, still feeling bad because he had been planning to stay at the house until Hayes had told him about me.

"You're worrying for nothing," he assured me, placing his palm on my lower back to lead me into the garage. "He just doesn't want me to kick his ass for hearing something that he shouldn't. You shouting my name as you come is for my ears only."

Climbing into the passenger seat of his SUV, I rolled my eyes. But I didn't bother arguing because I couldn't deny being loud in bed. So it probably was for the best that Nathan didn't stay with us the first time I met him.

What really helped settle my nerves was being

surrounded by the women of the Iron Rogues in the suite at the arena. I had already been well on my way to becoming good friends with Molly, Dahlia, and Elise before I met Hayes, and the time I spent at the Iron Rogues compound had solidified those relationships. I'd also gotten close with the others, and it felt good knowing they had my back if Nathan disapproved of me being with his brother.

Especially since he looked fierce out there on the ice.

"I had no idea hockey moved so fast."

"You shoulda seen me play." Hayes gently bumped his hip against me. "My kid brother is good, but I was better until that last injury took me outta the game."

"Don't worry." I beamed a smile at him. "I might not be familiar with ice hockey, but I don't need to see you play to know that you're my favorite player of all time."

"Damn straight, angel," he murmured before taking a sip of his beer.

I tugged on the sleeve of the jersey he was wearing. "I have to admit, I was surprised to see you in this. Although you're here to watch your brother, you played for the Trojans for years. Do your old teammates and fans give you a hard time for so publicly rooting for the competition?"

"Doesn't really matter." He shrugged and gestured toward the ice with his bottle of beer. "Nathan's family, and that's all that counts. I would have worn his jersey for him when I was still playing for the Trojans if my contract had allowed it. As long as my team wasn't the one facing off against him, I rooted for the Navigators."

His steadfast loyalty was just one of many traits making me fall head over heels in love with Hayes. "He's lucky to have a big brother like you. I enjoyed being an only child, but listening to you talk about him makes me think that I would have liked having an older sibling to look out for me."

"Nathan was a pain in my ass growing up, but I wouldn't trade him for anything." He wagged his brows at me over the rim of his beer bottle. "Maybe having three kids instead of two would make it easier on them when they're young. What do you think?"

"Um...not sure I'm the best person to ask since I didn't have the chance to experience sibling rivalry up close and personal like you."

"Three it is then."

Hayes had said similar stuff in the heat of the moment, but I hadn't been sure if he meant it. But the ease with which he casually mentioned us having a big family made my heart race. It also had me thinking about how he'd never used a condom any of the times we'd had sex. Which was a lot over the past week. And I wasn't on birth control.

Unfortunately, it was the wrong time and place to get into a serious discussion like that, even though we really should at some point when he wasn't already driving me out of my mind with desire.

"Remind me again why I couldn't borrow one of your Navigators jerseys?" I gestured at the green sweater I was wearing. "Instead of this? It's the team color, but I would've fit in with all the fans better if I was in their official gear. And you had five more just like the one you have on."

"Didn't want my brother's name on your back."

Reaching up to trace the letters on the back of his jersey, I pointed out, "But it's the same as yours."

"But the number under it is his, not mine," he growled. "I love Nathan, but no way in hell am I gonna have my woman walking around branded as his."

I hid my smile behind my drink, happy to know that I wasn't the only one in this relationship who was feeling possessive. Not that Hayes needed to worry—he was the only man I wanted.

His attention shifted to the ice, his blue eyes tracking his brother as he stole the puck from another guy's stick and skated toward the net.

We celebrated the goal with a kiss and ended up on the giant screens lining the stands. Hayes didn't seem bothered by it and claimed my lips again, only lifting his head when the crowd cheered. We glanced down at the ice to see Nathan pointing his stick at the box we were in, pumping his fist in the air.

"Oops," I giggled, my cheeks heating as I wondered if he was upset that we'd taken attention away from his goal.

Since we were already in the third period, I didn't have long before I found out. After the final buzzer rang and the teams left the ice, we said our goodbyes to everyone and headed down to meet Nathan. We spent about half an hour surrounded by women who didn't look like they'd dressed for a hockey game—puck bunnies, as Hayes explained.

With him leaning against the wall, his arms wrapped around me, and my back pressed against his chest, none of the women paid any attention to us. But they sure did perk up each time a player came out. Except none of them approached Nathan when he finally came through the doors, his dark hair still wet from his shower.

"Huh, that's weird," I mumbled.

"Them?" Hayes asked, jerking his chin toward the crowd. When I nodded, he explained, "They know it's not gonna do any good, so they don't bother. My brother followed my lead and trained the puck bunnies to stay away."

I beamed a smile at him, loving that he hadn't taken advantage of his professional athlete status to mess around with a bunch of women.

"Welcome to the family, Marnie." Instead of greeting his brother, Nathan headed straight for me and gave me a hug. But it didn't last long before Hayes yanked him away from me.

Sliding his arm around my shoulders, he grumbled, "Get your own girl."

Nathan cocked a brow. "You know what Mom and Dad have always said...sharing is caring."

"Never gonna happen." Hayes pulled me closer. "And I'd hate for Mom to cry because I had to make you bleed."

Nathan chuckled, shaking his head as he grinned at his brother. "Figured you'd say something along those lines, but I still had to yank your chain. That's what younger brothers are for, right?"

"Fucking hell." Hayes shook his head with a sigh.

"Let me know if this big lug doesn't do right by

you." Nathan winked at me, earning himself a half-punch to the shoulder from Hayes. "I'll kick his ass for you."

Hayes was proven right yet again. I didn't need to be worried about meeting Nathan. Although the way he welcomed me into their family did make me wonder what Hayes had told him about me.

Hayes and I had been together pretty much twenty-four seven for the past week and a half, but this was our first chance to go out on a real date. He hadn't given me any clues as to what he'd planned for our night, except that I needed to dress warm and in pants. I'd guessed about a dozen different things, but not once had I thought he'd rented out an entire ice rink so we'd have the place to ourselves while he taught me how to skate.

The only staff here when we arrived was the Zamboni driver, who'd assured Hayes the ice had been freshly cleared, and the guy working the snack bar. After he'd served us a dozen things from the menu, he'd headed out the door behind his coworker.

"I'm probably going to be really bad at this," I

warned Hayes as he laced up the skates he'd put on my feet.

Tilting his head back, he flashed me a cocky smirk. "Then it'll be a good thing you've got your very own pro to teach you."

"I guess," I conceded with a sigh.

After he finished with my skates, he straightened and held out a hand. I slid my mitten-covered palm against his and stood. My knees were wobbly, but it didn't take much effort on his part to help me hobble over to the open door. He stepped on the ice first, and waited for me to get my footing before he moved us away from the wall.

"You're doing good."

I rolled my eyes at his unwarranted compliment and clutched his arms even tighter. "Only because I have you to hold. Otherwise, I'd stick to the wall so I could keep a hand on it as I inched around the ice at a snail's pace."

"Thanks for going out of your comfort zone for me, angel." He glided backward on the ice, not even needing to look behind him to know that we needed to curve around the bend of the rink.

"Well, you did bribe me with a ton of delicious food." I smacked my lips. "I'm definitely going to need another walking taco the next time we go to a game."

"You got it," he promised.

"And a churro," I added, making him laugh.

We continued along at a slow pace for ten more minutes before he asked, "Wanna go faster?"

"Only if I can keep holding you for dear life."

"Always," he agreed with a grin.

He picked up the pace, and I enjoyed the glide of the ice beneath my skates and the breeze against my cheeks as I returned his smile.

"Are you shaking because you're scared?" he asked, looking down at me as we rounded the rink.

"No, I didn't realize ice was so cold," I laughed, shaking my head. "I mean, obviously it's cold to touch. But I didn't think I'd freeze my butt off skating."

"Let me warm you up."

He spun around, his arms going around my waist as he pulled me flush against his body. Tipping my chin so I was forced to look into his eyes, he was gentle, only briefly brushing his lips against mine.

But I didn't need gentle. I wanted everything Hayes had to give me.

Wrapping my arms around his neck, I pulled his

lips back to mine, sliding my tongue between his lips, trusting him to keep me upright.

His chest rumbled as he laughed against me, shaking my body.

"My greedy angel," he whispered into my lips.

"Always," I said, taking his lips back with mine.

He briefly broke our kiss with a laugh. "You want me to take you right here on the rink, angel?"

I shivered, looking at the ice. "Well, it might be a little cold."

He grinned, lifting me in the air like I was nothing.

"What are you doing?" I squealed as he skated us toward the edge and placed me on the other side of the short wall.

"Here? On the bench?" I asked.

He grinned, stepping over the wall until he was in front of me. Then he lifted me again and turned to perch me on the wall. He didn't say anything as he slid between my legs, wrapping his hands in my hair as he pulled me closer, kissing me fiercely. I moaned into his mouth, tasting everything he put into the kiss.

I didn't notice the cold anymore, my legs instinctively wrapping around him and pulling him close to me, already feeling his aching dick pressing against my core.

"I've dreamed of fucking you here ever since I kneeled in front of you to tie your skates," he murmured as his lips trailed down my neck.

I froze, not just from the cold but from his words.

"Then take me, Hayes," I whispered, cupping his hard dick through his jeans. "Right here. Right now."

He laughed. "Always my greedy angel."

Leaning back slightly, he shucked off his jacket, keeping one hand on me as he unbuttoned my jeans.

"How is this going to work?" I asked, looking up at his half-hooded eyes.

"Don't worry, angel, I've got you."

With one hand still wrapped around me, he used the other to strip off my jeans. My panties were the only thing covering my pussy as the cold air hit my skin, leaving goose bumps to spread down my legs.

"I'd better warm you up," he whispered, running his fingers over my drenched pussy.

He moaned. "Fuck, you're always so wet for me, angel."

I didn't care about the cold anymore as he slid his hand beneath the lacy fabric and pushed his fingers inside me, his thumb grazing my aching clit.

"You feel so good against my fingers. Come for

me, angel. Let me hear you scream my name in this rink. Just for me," he commanded, pumping his fingers harder against my core.

I gripped hard onto his shoulders, meeting his rhythm with his hips until my entire body shook as my orgasm took over.

"Oh, yes, Hayes," I yelled, the sounds of my orgasm echoing through the empty rink.

"Damn, that's so fucking hot," he growled before pulling me close and crushing his lips to mine.

As our tongues danced, I moved my hands between us, undoing his belt and jeans, letting them fall to the ground with a thud. He laughed against my lips as he pulled down his boxers and fisted his hard length in his free hand.

"You ready to make my fantasy a reality, angel?"

"Yes, please."

He pushed in slowly, but I pressed closer, ready for him to fill me.

The angle of his dick and my position on the wall was perfect for his hard ridges to rub against my clit as he thrust in and out of me.

"Oh, Hayes," I moaned, gripping hard onto his shoulders and pushing my body closer to him.

"Fuck, angel, your tight little pussy feels so amazing on my cock."

"You're hitting me just right," I moaned as my legs shook around him. "So good. I'm already close again."

"You gonna give me another one, angel? Scream my name again while your pussy clenches around my big dick?"

His dirty talk was exactly what I needed to push me over the edge. My orgasm exploded, making me see stars as my entire body vibrated around him.

"Yeah, that's it, angel, come all over my cock," he growled, pumping harder into me.

"Now open those legs and lean back. 'Cause you're gonna take all of my come, angel."

I'd never really thought about kids or the future before. But with him, I could see it all. Even Saturdays at rinks like this with a brood of hockey-playing sons, and I'd probably blush every time I saw the bench.

"Come for me again, angel. I want to feel you as I fill this pussy," he commanded, sliding his hand between us and circling my hardened nub.

I met his pace as a third orgasm took hold. I screamed out, my entire body on fire as I rode out the wave yet again.

"Fuck, that's it, my angel," he growled as his

body stilled against mine, his hot spurts shooting into my swollen core.

I could barely catch my breath as I gripped his shoulders, feeling the steady beat of his heart against my chest.

We stayed just like that, holding each other for a few beats before he cupped my face, kissing my lips lightly. "Thanks for being my fantasy, angel."

I laughed. "Thanks for giving me a fantasy I didn't even know I had."

Including the one that involved my belly round with his baby. Something that was bound to happen sooner than later if we kept on going at each other like this without any protection.

10

ICE

My phone rang as Marnie and I walked out of the salon after her shift. While she locked up, I glanced at the screen and saw that it was my prez calling, so I answered immediately.

"Fox," I greeted. "I'm with Marnie." I let him know in case he was calling about club business and I needed to get my angel in the car before we talked.

"Something's come up. We think it involves Franks."

Hearing that name, my grip on my cell tightened as I ground my teeth together. "Tell me."

"Better if you come here so we can show you and talk. It involves Marnie, but it's up to you whether she knows or not."

I wasn't gonna drag her into this unless I had to.

"Gonna take her home before I meet you. Send a prospect out to watch the house, would you?"

"Done." He hung up, and I dropped my phone back into the inner pocket of my cut and threaded my fingers through Marnie's before leading her over to my SUV.

When I'd met my angel, I hadn't needed any transportation other than my hog. But now, I not only had Marnie to think about, but we'd soon be toting around our little ones if I had my way. So a few days after we met, I had one of the safest SUVs on the market delivered to the compound. It had taken a little time to get it because I'd ordered one that was bullet proof and had other security measures to keep my family from harm.

"Fox needs to meet with me," I explained once we were both in our seats and buckled in.

"I gathered that. Is it club business?"

I wanted to lie and say that it was so she wouldn't ask any more questions. As if my angel wasn't perfect enough, she'd come to me after hanging with the old ladies one day and told me they'd given her a rundown of life with an MC man. She'd said she was fine with not knowing club business as long as I was honest with her about everything else.

So I was gonna keep my word. I mulled over my

answer as I started the car, then said, "Probably not, but I can't be sure that it won't go in that direction. You'll just have to trust me to tell you if you need to be involved, okay?"

"I do trust you," she affirmed.

Warmth spread through me at her declaration, and I took her hand, lacing my fingers through hers and resting them on my thigh.

I expected her to go on, but she was quiet for so long that I glanced at her, worried she was upset and trying to hide it. But she watched me with a thoughtful expression, her brow lowered and her teeth nibbling on her lower lip. I forced my attention back to the road, so I kept my mouth shut and waited for her to speak.

Finally, she murmured, "Just promise me that you won't let your overprotective streak drive a wedge between us. You can tell me anything. It won't scare me away. I'm stronger than I look."

I brought our joined hands up to my mouth and brushed a kiss over the back of hers. "I promise."

We'd reached our house, so I waited until I pulled into our driveway and parked before saying anything else. I unbuckled both of us, then grabbed her waist and hauled her into my lap so she straddled me.

I tunneled my fingers into her thick, silky hair and held her head steady so she was forced to look straight into my eyes. "If I didn't think you could handle being my woman, I would have walked away from you the day we met. No matter how much I wanted you in my bed. But I knew, angel. Knew you were perfect for me. Strong enough, and stubborn enough, to deal with the bad shit along with the good." I grinned and winked at her. "Knew that underneath all your sweetness was a wild streak that would make you a firecracker in bed."

Marnie's cheeks turned pink, and I laughed before planting a kiss on her soft, supple lips. "Somehow, you manage to be cute and sexy as hell at the same time. Don't know how you do it, but it's a lethal combination. Makes me want to cuddle you and fuck you hard and fast all at once."

The blush staining her skin deepened, but fire sparked in her green depths, and she moved restlessly on top of me.

I groaned when her pussy rubbed my swollen cock. "Need to get you in the house before I take you right here."

Marnie's voice was breathless when she quipped, "You say that as though it's a bad thing."

Shaking my head, I picked her up and gently set

her back in her seat. "First, if anyone saw you while I was fucking you, I'd end up in jail for murder. Second, I don't have time." I grabbed her chin and smirked when our eyes met. "But the minute I get home, you'll be screaming in ecstasy until you pass out."

"I guess you'd better hurry then, shouldn't you?" she sassed before opening her door and stepping down onto the runners I'd put on so my tiny angel wouldn't get hurt jumping down from the car.

Her hips had an extra sway in them as she sashayed to the front door, and I growled in frustration. And pain, since I was hard as fuck and the zipper in my leather pants scraped my dick. I really needed to start wearing underwear before I ended up with permanent marks from the metal teeth on my cock. Just thinking about my angel had my dick ready to fuck.

When Marnie reached the front door, she unlocked it, then pivoted, making sure her curtain of hair swung around and landed on her tits. Then she twirled her fingers in the soft curls that I was so obsessed with and blinked up at me with false innocence. "Don't be too long, or I just might have to start without you."

Another growl rumbled in my chest as I leaned

around her and twisted the knob, then used my hand on her stomach to push her inside.

Once the door was shut, I fisted my hands in her hair on both sides of her head and lowered my head until our faces were millimeters apart. "You're dangerously close to earning a spanking, angel. That's my pussy, and nobody but me touches it. Not even you."

Marnie gasped, but I didn't give her a chance to say anything. I kissed her hard and turned back to open the front door. "Set the alarm when I'm gone, angel."

I stepped outside and turned back to pull the door closed behind me, but I paused and met her heated gaze. "Remember, you touch my pussy and your ass will be cherry red. You won't be able to sit down tomorrow without remembering who owns it."

Marnie's green orbs darkened to nearly black, and I gritted my teeth when I realized that the idea of being spanked was turning her on. I slammed the door shut before I gave in to my urge to fuck her against the wall.

This had better be fucking worth it, I thought as I stomped back to the car.

I was still in a foul mood when I entered Fox's office fifteen minutes later. Maverick leaned against the wall behind Fox's desk, the two of them in deep discussion.

"Am I gonna get to kill that fucker?" I snarled as I stalked over to the couch and dropped onto it.

Mav turned his head and peered over at me. "Maybe."

I perked up at his answer, having expected the opposite response.

"Unlikely," Fox grunted, leaning back in his chair and crossing his arms over his chest.

Glaring at Mav, I grumbled, "Don't give me false hope when this asshole just pulled me away from my woman and our bed."

My attention was diverted when a couple more enforcers walked into the room. Deviant was our resident tech genius, and Stone had been a lawyer before joining the Iron Rogues. He quit seeing other clients once he patched, choosing to only use those skills for the club.

Stone stalked over to the sitting area and plopped down into a chair across from me. His expression was grim as he leaned forward and tossed a stack of papers in front of me.

I picked it up and frowned as I scanned the document, confused as to why I was looking at an insurance policy.

"Why am—" I stopped when I got to the name of the insured. "What the fuck?"

"This can't be real."

"It's legit," Stone muttered. "Marnie took out an insurance policy on you."

"Bullshit," I spat.

Stone held up his hand and shook his head. "I said that wrong. I meant that someone pretending to be Marnie took out an insurance policy on you. But I gotta say, it's a damn good forgery. I'm not sure we can even prove it wasn't her."

"Better find a fucking way," I growled. Snatching up the papers, I scanned the first page. "You think Franks did this?"

"He wants that property, and apparently, he's figured out that it will only happen over your dead body," Deviant piped up from the loveseat pushed up against my right.

"Look on page seven," Stone urged.

I flipped through the stack until I found it. A cursory glance told me why Stone had directed me to that page. "You have to be fucking kidding me."

"Nope. Everything goes to her unless your death is declared a homicide and the beneficiary is a suspect. Then all of your assets will go into a trust. If she's convicted, or anything else happens to her, then the trustee will control everything."

"Not seeing how this all fits together," I muttered, shuffling through the rest of the documents.

"Take a look at the name of the trustee," Deviant suggested.

"Sam Frankel?"

Deviant had opened a laptop he'd brought with him and after a few clicks, he set it on the low coffee table in front of me. "It took some digging, but I eventually connected the dots and got my hands on the legal paperwork for the name change."

"Keith Franks used to be Sam Frankel?"

Deviant nodded. "He legally changed it when he was eighteen, but he still uses his old surname as an alias. I hate to admit this about that motherfucker, but he was smart and kept the two names completely unrelated to each other." Then he shrugged, and his lips lifted cockily at the corners. "I'm just smarter."

"Okay. So it's clear that Franks intends to get rid of me," I conceded. "But Marnie would still be in control of my assets."

Fox sighed, drawing my focus over to his desk. "He either intends to frame her or..."

"I'll kill him!" I roared, shooting to my feet.

Knowing someone wanted my angel dead built a fury inside me that had my vision going red, my blood boiling, and my hands itching for a weapon. I wasn't just going to kill that motherfucker. First, I was gonna make him bleed and scream for mercy.

"Sit the fuck down," Fox ordered, cutting through the fog of rage surrounding me.

I was tempted to ignore his directive, but I respected my prez and had agreed to follow him when I patched, so I lowered myself to the couch again. My hands rested on my knees, clenching and unclenching as I tried to remain calm.

"I sent Whiskey, Viper, and Wrecker to watch over her when I asked you to come here," Fox assured me. Though it didn't make me feel much better. I wanted Marnie in my eyesight at all times.

"Wasn't sure how much you wanted her to know and figured it would be best if you made the decision before you saw her again."

"Been looking for a loophole in the paperwork since we found it," Stone interjected. "Haven't found one yet, but nobody is perfect. He'll have made a mistake somewhere."

"I'm working on connecting his aliases," Deviant said as he reached out for his computer and set it on his lap. "Sam Frankel technically no longer exists, so Stone's working on those angles, too."

"Basically, you're telling me to sit and wait," I concluded, my body practically vibrating with the need to expend some of the energy building from the anger inside me.

"Nah," Maverick said with a smirk. "Here's where the possible killing comes in."

I raised an eyebrow, waiting for his explanation.

"Mav," Fox sighed.

The VP looked at him with a hard expression. "If it were Dahlia?"

Fox's whole body tensed, and something lethal sparked in his eyes. "Point taken. Still say it's a bad idea, but I won't stand in your way." Then he smirked at Mav and drawled, "But you're making the call."

Maverick sighed, then nodded before turning his gaze back to me. "Give Stone and Deviant a day to come up with something. If they do, we'll make sure Franks pays for his shit once he's in a cell."

Not my first choice, but certainly the one with the least risk of being taken away from my angel. "And if they don't find a solution?"

"Rumor is that Franks took money from the

Mafia to start his business and is behind on his payments."

"The DeLucas?" I asked, finding that hard to believe.

Nic DeLuca was the head of the New York Mafia, and though he mostly didn't interfere in their business, he still held a lot of power over pretty much every "family" in the United States. He'd also been friends with Fox for decades and a client of ours since Fox became our prez.

Other than being a criminal and ruthless killer, he had honor and integrity—something he had in common with the Iron Rogues. So I couldn't see him getting into bed with scum like Franks.

"It's just a rumor," Mav clarified. "But most people think it's true. So I doubt even the cops would be surprised if—"

"You want to make it look like a mob hit," I deduced.

Mav nodded, an evil grin splitting his face. "Long as DeLuca's on board."

My brow shot up, suddenly understanding Fox's comment about Mav making the call.

"Making a deal with Nic DeLuca?" Deviant commented with a whistle. "You got some balls, man."

"What makes you think he'll agree to do this for you?" I asked. "Prez, sure. But if he isn't willing to get involved..."

"Anna," Mav said simply, referring to Nic's wife.

Suddenly, I understood his confidence. Just like Fox caved when Maverick brought up his old lady, Nic would understand my need to protect my woman.

"And we'll owe him a favor," Maverick added.

I could see how that would be appealing to the Mafia boss.

There was something I didn't understand, though. "Why the elaborate scheme? Why not just make him disappear?" We'd certainly done it before.

"Franks is more high profile and is always in the media. Even though he's an asshole and I doubt anyone will miss him, it's asking a lot of our police to look the other way on this one. We'll need 'em in the future, and I don't want them getting skittish."

I nodded in understanding. We had a good portion of the police force in our small town on the payroll, as well as the mayor, but they still answered to higher authorities. While they were often willing to overlook our activities, they wouldn't break the law for us. Something we respected.

"So my options are owing a powerful crime

family a favor in order to put Franks six feet under or sit back and wait, leaving Marnie vulnerable while Stone and Deviant look for a less messy solution."

"That about sums it up," Fox agreed.

For me, there was nothing to consider. I was gonna choose whatever kept Marnie the safest, which meant taking out Franks.

I scrubbed my hands over my face and exhaled heavily. "Looks like we're making a call to the DeLucas," I murmured.

Maverick nodded and pulled his phone from his pocket, pausing when I shook my head.

I stood and held out my hand. "I appreciate you being willing, but if anyone is gonna owe Nic DeLuca for this, it's gonna be me."

Maverick looked at Fox, who was considering me thoughtfully.

"Your woman, your decision," Prez told me. "You can use my office."

Once everyone had cleared the room, I sat behind Fox's desk and looked at my phone. I hadn't wanted to use Maverick's, so he'd given me Nic's private number.

I hit send and put the phone to my ear. It rang twice before a deep voice answered tersely.

"DeLuca. Who the fuck is this?"

I wasn't surprised at his reception, considering someone he didn't recognize was calling his private line.

"Name's Ice. I'm an enforcer with the Iron Rogues."

"Ice, huh?" His voice had become much more congenial, though it was still wary. "You're going to have to explain that one. If it's because you're a cold-blooded killer, I must insist on stealing you from Fox to come work for me."

I chuckled. "Don't you call him Kye?"

Nic was silent for a moment, then his tone became even friendlier when he replied, "*Molto bene*." Then he asked me a few more probing and annoying questions that he obviously believed would prove that I was who I claimed to be.

"Satisfied?" I asked dryly.

Nic laughed. "You know I was just fucking with you, right? Kye sent me a text letting me know you'd be calling."

"Figures." I rolled my eyes but couldn't help chuckling. And I was grateful that Fox had paved the way for me.

"He didn't explain your road name, though."

"Former pro hockey player for the Tennessee Trojans," I explained. "It's in my blood somewhere because my brother plays center for the New York Navigators." I paused, then gave him the full truth because, why the hell not? "And my empathy could use some work."

"I think I like you, Ice," Nic chuckled.

"Good. Then you won't mind doing me a favor."

He was silent for a few beats, then said, "I'm listening."

I quickly laid out the whole situation and Maverick's plan. "All we need is your permission to lead the investigation toward the local, nonexistent branch of The Family. And if they come calling, you can prove that you have no contact with this so-called Mafia family—"

"And therefore confirm their existence," Nic finished.

"Exactly. And if needed, we'll have our guys on the force lead the investigation in another direction."

"Why would I do this for you?"

I hesitated, unsure of what angle I wanted to play. "I'll owe you."

"You'll owe me," he confirmed.

"Yes." I tried not to let my irritation seep into my tone, but I knew I'd failed when he laughed.

"That's your play here?"

Again, I hesitated, thinking about Maverick's plan...but I didn't want to go there unless it was my last resort. "Yes. That's my pitch."

"Hmm, to be honest, you're not asking much. And if it were Kye, I would do it without the quid pro quo. But there is something I want from you."

"Already?" I hadn't expected him to call in his chips immediately.

"*Si.*"

"What is it?"

"Your brother."

"Excuse me?"

"Your brother is Nathan Gallagher, *corretto*?"

"Yes. What could you possibly want with Nathan?"

"As it happens, my son is obsessed with hockey, and he is a huge fan of your brother. I have connections, but they only get me perks at the stadium unless I'm willing to use...let's call it underhanded techniques. I try not to resort to that outside of my business."

"I understand."

"If you'll ask your brother to come to dinner and spend a couple of hours with my son, I'll make sure your problem is handled."

"You want my brother to come to dinner?" I asked incredulously, not trusting that it could be this simple.

"That's it. I'll be my son's hero. When you have kids, you'll understand the magnitude of that."

"I can imagine," I murmured, thinking about a dark-haired, green-eyed little baby and hoping that Marnie was already carrying our son or daughter.

"Do we have a deal?"

"I'll have Nathan call you."

"*Bene.* Oh, I have one more condition. *Mi dispiace*, I should have mentioned it earlier."

My brow furrowed at the serious note in his voice.

"In order for this to work, you'll have to let my man take out your target."

"What the fuck?" I growled. "You're asking me to step back and let someone else dispose of the man threatening my woman?"

"I understand your need for vengeance and to be the one to cause this asshole pain, but in order for this to work, you need a trail that doesn't lead back to you. One that my man knows how to leave to ensure it also disappears at the right moment."

"Nic—"

"I appreciate that you didn't use Gianna to coerce my agreement, Ice," he interrupted, throwing me off balance.

"You're welcome," I replied gruffly. "If it were me—"

"Exactly my point. If it were me. Even though you didn't use Gianna as a tactic, my mind still went there. And honestly, *amico*, as hard as it would be to step back from the situation, I would do it if it was what was best for my wife. Can you honestly tell me that removing yourself from the threat of suspicion isn't what is best for your woman?"

"Fucking hell," I muttered. He was right, but I was loath to admit it. "I don't know how Fox puts up with you."

"Trust me, he can be just as much of a cocky motherfucker as I can. Especially when he's right."

"True."

"I look forward to meeting your brother, Ice. And think about coming with him. You're welcome at my home any time."

His invitation was unexpected but very much appreciated, considering how tight he kept his circle. "Thank you. I just might do that."

"You'll hear from me soon."

The connection ended abruptly, and I leaned back in my chair, playing over our conversation and wondering how the man had talked me in circles.

I took a deep breath and shook my head, trying to clear my mind of everything except my angel. She was the only thing that would soothe my instincts to hunt Franks down and dismember him myself.

There was a knock on the door before it opened and Fox and Maverick walked into the room.

"So?" Maverick stuck his hands in his front pockets and cocked his head to the side. "Is he in?"

I put my palms flat on the desktop and pushed down, rising to my feet. "In a manner of speaking."

"What does that mean?"

"It means he agreed, but only if we do it his way," Fox supplied.

"Yeah."

Maverick frowned. "And his way is what?"

I shrugged. "Whatever way he wants. He'll call when it's done."

Fox studied me for a moment, then asked, "And you're okay with this?"

"Couldn't argue with his logic," I answered. "Letting him handle it keeps both Marnie and me safe. And that's what is most important."

Fox smiled approvingly, then his expression turned curious. "What did he want in return?"

I told them about Nic's request, and they both laughed. Then Fox ambled over and slapped me on the back. "Go home to your woman."

Glancing at my watch, I was happy to see I'd only been gone about an hour and a half. Which meant Marnie would still be awake, and I could make up for leaving so abruptly earlier.

I was almost to the door when Fox called out my name, and I halted, turning halfway around to see what he wanted.

He held up a vest. "Almost forgot. Sheila dropped it off earlier."

Fox tossed it to me, and I easily caught it, then held it up to look at the property patch taking up almost the entire back. Pride swelled in my chest, and my heart thumped. Yeah, I needed to be with my angel.

"You hear something from Nic, call," I told them. "Otherwise, don't bother me for a few days."

Ignoring their laughter, I turned and stalked from the room.

The ride home felt like hours, and relief washed over me when I saw Whiskey step out of the shadows and raise his chin in greeting as he walked toward me.

I quickly exited the car and glanced up at the house before meeting Whiskey's eyes.

"Everything's been quiet," he told me. "She's fine."

"Thanks," I murmured, and we shook hands. Viper and Wrecker rode up on their bikes, and I nodded to them in silent thanks, receiving the same gesture in return.

I walked through the front door when I heard the rumble of all three motorcycles as they headed down the road.

I put her vest in the coat closet for the time being, shutting the door just as Marnie came around the corner from the kitchen.

She beamed when she saw me. "You're home."

"C'mere," I ordered gruffly, holding out an arm. She hurried over, and I wrapped her in my embrace, rubbing my chin in her silky waves. "Fuck, I missed you."

She dropped her head back, and her eyes twinkled happily. "I missed you too. I made dinner, so I hope you're hungry."

"I am starving, angel," I grunted before sweeping her off her feet and stalking toward the stairs and up to our bedroom.

"But dinner..." Marnie gasped as I tossed her onto the bed, then laughed as she bounced on the mattress.

"What I'm craving is between your sexy thighs, angel."

JUST OVER TWENTY-FOUR HOURS LATER, I received a call from a number I didn't recognize, though it had a New York City area code.

"Tell me it's done," I said in lieu of a greeting.

"Turn on the news," Nic murmured, then hung up.

I was in my home office, catching up on some work, so I grabbed the remote to the TV mounted on the wall and hit the power button.

The local news channel blinked on, and Lonnie Damien, a rookie reporter, stood in front of a construction site.

"The victim has been identified as Keith Franks, a local land developer. He was shot execution-style with a single bullet to the back of the head."

Lonnie paused and put his finger to his ear, then straightened and looked directly into the camera, a grim expression on his face. He was overdoing it with the theatrics, but I didn't care as long as I heard what I wanted.

"Rumors that Franks was in bed with the local Mafia are swirling, and though police have declined to comment, I'm being told that there's evidence supporting this theory."

He paused again, then a flash of triumph crossed his face for a second before he could school it into his serious facade.

"New information has just come to light. It seems this man, Keith Franks, is in fact Sam Frankel, a man

the police have suspected is a hit man for The Family."

I chuckled, knowing that Stone and Deviant had obviously sent their research to Nic so they could build an even stronger case for the mob hit.

My phone pinged, and I glanced at it, seeing a message from Deviant.

DEVIANT

Damn, he's good.

I smiled and shot off a text to Nathan, telling him I needed a favor and to call when he had a chance.

NATHAN

Will do.

Marnie pushed open the door to my office just as I shut off the television.

"You look happy," she said with a sweet smile.

I held out my hand, and she rounded my desk, allowing me to pull her into my lap. "You are all I'll ever need to make me happy, angel," I told her softly. "But I did get some other good news."

"I love good news!" she chirped happily, making me laugh.

"The man targeting me is gone, and he won't be back. It's all over."

12

MARNIE

I stared into his icy-blue eyes, stunned by this sudden turn of events. "It's done? You don't have to worry about him anymore?"

"He's not gonna be a problem for either of us," he reassured me. "You can count on that, angel."

"I'm so glad you don't have to worry about someone sabotaging your bike like that again," I whispered, clutching his shoulders as I thought about how different my life would have been if that jerk had gotten what he'd wanted out of the accident— Hayes dead. "He deserves all of the bad karma he has coming his way."

"He can burn in hell for all I care, but he's not gonna get another minute of our attention." His hand stroked down my spine to cup my butt. "We've got better things to focus on."

Now that the dust had settled with the man who had it out for Hayes, I had to face the fear plaguing me since we first got together. Did he really see a future with me? Or had things moved so quickly between us because of the adrenaline of how we met?

"What happens next?"

His brows drew together at my question. "What do you mean?"

"Um, well...I have a lot of stuff at your house." I cleared the sudden lump in my throat. "But there's no longer danger of that guy coming after me for witnessing your accident. So..."

I was unable to get the words past my stiff lips. But Hayes got the point I was trying to make. And it pissed him off, judging by the angry gleam in his eyes.

"What the hell, angel?" he growled, his fingers digging into my hips as he yanked me closer. "Are you sitting on my lap, tryin' to tell me that you wanna move out of our home now that we don't have to worry about that asshole hurting you?"

I shook my head. "No, absolutely not."

"Then what the fuck were you trying to say?"

"You kinda already answered my question, which makes it easier to ask. If that makes any sense." I cupped his bearded cheeks. "Do you want me to stay even though I don't need to be here for my protection?"

"Fuck yeah, I do." His eyes narrowed. "Did you really doubt that'd be my answer?"

I shrugged. "You have to admit that things moved fast with us."

"Is that your only reason for thinking I didn't mean it each and every time I called you mine?" he demanded, grinding his hard-on against my core. "And not just when I was buried balls deep inside you. 'Cause I know damn well I've said it plenty of other times, too."

"You have," I confirmed, twining my arms around his neck as I relaxed in his hold. "But I've never been in a relationship before. So I didn't know how seriously I should take stuff like that when we've never labeled what's happened beyond me being yours and you being mine."

"You want me to be crystal clear about what we are to each other?" he asked.

"Uh-huh," I breathed with a nod.

He lifted me off his lap and set me in his chair. "Stay put. I'll be right back."

I practically held my breath as he stormed out of his office. My curiosity over what he was doing was quickly answered when he returned a moment later, carrying a smaller version of his vest in his fist. After rounding his desk, he crouched next to me, turning the leather so I could see the patch on the back that said "Property of Ice."

I beamed a big smile at him, sniffling as my eyes filled with tears. "You want me to be your old lady?"

"That and more," he confirmed, tugging me forward to slide my arms through the holes and settling the leather on my back. Then he captured my mouth in a deep kiss, clenching the front of my new vest to hold me in place.

When he finally lifted his head again, I blinked up at him. "What's more than your old lady? I thought that was the highest honor you could give a woman in the biker world."

"You're everything to me, Marnie." He yanked open the top drawer of his desk and pulled out a black jewelry box. Flipping open the lid with his thumb, he showed me the diamond solitaire nestled inside. Plucking it out of the black velvet between his thumb and index finger, he slid it onto my finger. "You're gonna spend the rest of your life being my old lady, my wife, and the mother of my children. I wanna build a family with you, me, and three babies that'll hopefully have your black hair and green eyes. That work for you?"

It wasn't the proposal that most women dreamed of, but Hayes basically telling me that we were getting married was perfect for me. "It does, but I have two tiny issues with the future you laid out for us."

"Only two?" he asked with a grin. "That's not too bad, considering. What are they?"

"I want at least one of our babies to have dark hair and pale blue eyes, just like their daddy."

His smile widened, and he nodded. "That'd work for me, but I guess we're gonna have to wait and see what we end up with. If the first three all look alike, we can keep on trying for another until we both have a mini-me."

I narrowed my eyes at him. "Is this your way of tricking me into having more than three kids?"

"You got a problem with the plan if that's what I'm doing?" he countered.

"Nah." I shook my head. "As long as you give me the right answer to my second question, I'm good with having as many babies as you want. Within reason."

"We'll negotiate what reason means after I've given you whatever you need so we can celebrate you being my old lady and fiancée." His palm settled over my flat belly. "And maybe even get to work on that first baby if you're not already pregnant."

I hadn't had a period since I met Hayes, but it wasn't due for a couple more days. The timing wasn't likely for him to knock me up today, but that wouldn't stop me from letting him try as often as he'd like. After he'd alleviated my other concern.

"Do you love me?"

"Fuck, angel," he rasped, standing before pulling me to my feet. "I can't believe I haven't said it yet. I love you so damn much. More than I ever thought possible."

"Really?" I cried, pressing trembling fingers to my lips.

"I fell for you hard and fast." He shook his head with a rueful laugh. "Probably started from the moment I opened my eyes after my accident and saw you standing over me. My beautiful angel."

"I love you, too," I confessed, pressing my face against his chest.

"Good, because you're stuck with me, Marnie Miller, soon-to-be Gallagher."

It turned out that he hadn't been kidding when he said soon...we got married only four days later. Hours after we found out that I was already pregnant.

EPILOGUE
ICE

"I don't like seeing you so exhausted after work," I grumbled as I led my wife out to the car. She'd just finished a six-hour shift and looked dead on her feet. Which were now even bigger since they'd swelled lately due to her pregnancy.

Marnie sighed. "I know. I'll try to take a few more breaks, okay?"

Attempting to talk her into quitting had only resulted in arguments, and I didn't like upsetting her. Although, I had no complaints about the makeup sex.

I knew she loved her work, but it would only get harder with a baby, especially when she got pregnant again. So I'd taken matters into my own hands and had a surprise for her.

Once we were in the car and headed home, I picked up the conversation again. "Would be a fuck of a lot easier if your clients came to you. And you had a place to take a nap between appointments."

"Ideally, yes. But I'm not going to open a competing salon in town just so I can put a nap room in the back."

I grinned and captured her hand, resting it on my thigh. "I think I came up with a better solution."

"Oh? What is it?"

"You'll just have to wait and see," I told her with a quick wink in her direction.

Marnie huffed and crossed her arms over her protruding belly, which pushed up her tits and distracted me for a second. They'd grown bigger and more sensitive since I knocked her up. My dick hardened at memories of making her come just by playing with her sexy globes.

"I hate surprises," she complained.

I barked a laugh. "No, you don't. You're just too impatient to wait for them."

"If you already know that, then you're just being mean."

My eyes narrowed, and I glanced over at her. "Are you trying to get spanked, angel?"

Marnie squirmed in her seat and whispered, "No," with a little too much innocence.

"Not as effective if you're begging for it," I muttered. "Maybe next time, I'll redden your cute little ass without letting you come."

"You wouldn't," she gasped.

"Try me."

She said nothing at first, then snapped, "Fine. I'll wait patiently."

"Good girl," I crooned, taking her hand once more. "Only gotta wait a few more minutes anyway."

We drove up to our house, and I parked at the curb in front because caution tape blocked the driveway. A brand-new portion had been added that morning, and it extended around the corner of the house, leading to a small lot that would hold another three cars.

"You widened the driveway?" she asked, her brow furrowed in confusion. "Are you planning to start throwing a bunch of big parties?"

I laughed and shook my head as I opened the door and exited the vehicle. Quickly rounding the hood, I went to her door to help her out of the SUV. Even with the runners, it was a big step to the ground. Her baby bump was throwing her balance a little off lately, and I didn't want to risk her falling.

"Nothing other than an occasional barbecue with the club."

"Then why—"

"You'll see." I interrupted, putting her arm through mine and guiding her around the house.

Her eyebrows shot to her hairline when she saw a new door leading into the house. "What is that?" she asked incredulously. "You added a door to the outside in the new playroom?"

"Not just a playroom, angel," I told her with a sly grin.

I pulled a key out of my pocket and opened the door, ushering her inside.

She stopped and gasped as she looked around, seeing how the space was set up.

"You...you built me a salon in our house?"

"Now, you can rest in our bed when you need to and get real food from the kitchen when you're hungry."

"But..." She looked up at me with conflicting emotions in her beautiful green orbs. "This is amazing, Hayes. But you promised to always be honest with me."

Her eyes filled with tears, and I mentally kicked myself for forgetting how emotional she'd been lately. The pregnancy hormones made her cry at the tiniest things, and I hated it when she cried.

She'd known something was going on in this part of the house, but I'd managed to keep my surprise hidden by telling her that I was having a new play-room built. Since it was a construction zone, I had the perfect excuse for keeping her out of the space. Too many hazards. But while I'd omitted part of the purpose for the construction, I hadn't lied either.

"I didn't break my promise, angel," I replied softly, guiding her across the room to another door.

There were tall windows in the wall on both sides of the entry, but the shades were down so she couldn't see what was behind them.

I opened the door and gestured for her to walk in first. "Oh my gosh!" she exclaimed, and to my relief, excitement replaced her sadness.

The room looked like a simpler version of some-thing you would find in one of those play places with the tunnels, trampolines, and even a shallow ball pit. There was also a little area surrounded by a short wall and a gate with a shelf full of toddler and baby toys. Across from that was a little reading nook with two empty bookshelves I knew she would enjoy filling.

"Now you have a place for our little ones to play

if you have an appointment and I can't be home. And any clients with kids can bring them so that you can have a more flexible schedule."

I walked over to the tall, wide windows and pushed up the cordless shades. "I wanted to make sure that you and your clients had a clear view of the kids playing, but you can drop the shades if you want to put one of them down for a nap."

"Hayes," she breathed, hurrying over to stand in front of me. "This is amazing. I can't believe you did this for me."

I delved my hands into her silky dark tresses and held her head in place. Staring into her amazing eyes, I murmured, "You should know by now, angel. I'd do anything for you. I love you more than anything."

"I love you so much, Hayes," she uttered in a thick voice as moisture gathered in her eyes.

"Don't you dare cry," I scolded, scowling at her.

"Then stop doing sweet things," she wailed as the tears tracked down her cheeks.

"Fucking hell," I groaned. "Guess I'm gonna have to distract you."

I gently tugged her out into the main area and over to the chair where she'd work on her clients.

"Distract me?"

"Yup. Gonna fuck you right here. You're gonna

ride my cock until you're screaming my name. Then you'll think about that every time you look at it."

It took Marnie two weeks of seeing clients in her new salon before she could look at that chair without blushing.

EPILOGUE

MARNIE

Having three children under the age of five wasn't always easy, but I wouldn't trade it for anything. The family Hayes and I were building meant everything to me. Even when I'd only had about a dozen hours of sleep over the past three days.

"I'm not sure how it's possible, but my tired is tired." I heaved a deep sigh as I planted face-first on our mattress. "Whose bright idea was it for us to have our three children so close together? Because I don't remember the last time I had a full night's sleep."

"Mine," Hayes admitted, stroking his palm down my back after he dropped down next to me. "But you agreed each time. Enthusiastically, from what I remember."

Rolling to my side, I flashed him an exhausted

smile. "I can't deny that, but those memories feel like they're from so long ago."

"I just had you screaming my name this afternoon while the kids were down for their nap," he reminded me, his hand moving lower to cup my butt cheek.

I lifted off the mattress to arch into his touch. "Now, that I do remember."

"You better." He leaned down to press a kiss against the back of my neck. "I'd hate to think having my cock deep inside your pussy was forgettable."

"Never," I swore, turning onto my back. "But I might need a reminder of how it feels when you're trying to knock me up."

"Are you sayin' what I think you're sayin'?" he asked, gripping my hips as he rolled onto his back, settling me on top of him.

Pressing my knees into the mattress on either side of his hips, I grinned down at him. "Yeah."

"You want me to put another baby in your belly?" he growled. "'Cause I'm down for that."

"I know." I laughed softly, stroking my hands up his chest. "I might be exhausted chasing our little hellions, but I still caught the hints you've been dropping lately. You weren't exactly subtle."

"Have you ever known me to be?" he teased, a wicked gleam in his icy-blue eyes.

"Nope, not even a little bit." I bent low to brush my lips against his and whispered, "It's one of the things I love best about you. That I never have to guess where I stand with you because you're always up front about what you want. And you show me how much you love the kids and me every single day."

"You really want to make our terrible trio into a ferocious foursome?"

"Yeah," I confirmed, grinding down against his hard length. "If I'm lucky, I'll get another mini-you to chase. Hank could use a brother to go with his pair of sisters."

I got what I wanted when I gave birth to our first child, but then Hayes got two little girls who were mirror images of me. Michelle and Marie were handfuls, even more than their big brother. Probably because they had their daddy wrapped around their little fingers. The girls could do no wrong as far as he was concerned. Not even when they used my bright red nail polish on his motorcycle.

"I'll give it my all, angel."

He didn't waste any time getting down to business, quickly stripping us out of our clothes before pressing me back onto the mattress and crawling between my legs. Wedging his shoulders between my thighs, he lowered his head and dragged his tongue up my center.

"Oh yes," I cried, threading my fingers through his thick hair to press his face closer to my core.

He ate me through two orgasms before getting to his knees and notching the tip of his dick at my center. His pale blue eyes were heated as he stared down at me, gripping my hips to pull me down his length until he was lodged balls deep inside me.

He never looked away as he picked up the pace, thrusting hard enough that I had to stretch my hands out to hold the headboard while he worked his cock in and out of my pussy. Over and over again until we were both near the edge.

"You feel so damn good, angel. I swear, your pussy keeps sucking me back in because it doesn't want to let my big cock go."

"Because I don't," I gasped as he changed the angle to hit me in a different spot.

"You gonna come all over my dick?" he grunted, wedging his arm between us to circle my clit with his thumb.

"Yes," I hissed.

"That's it, angel. Fuck, yes. Fuck! Squeeze that

tight little pussy and milk the come from my cock. Wanna knock you up tonight."

I threw my head back, punching my hips up to meet his every thrust. "Yes! Oh, yes! Hayes!"

Fireworks went off behind my eyelids, and my inner walls clenched around his shaft. Hayes bellowed as he exploded inside me, jets of hot come filling me up. Then he collapsed on top of me, careful to keep most of his weight on his elbows.

"Damn, angel," he groaned. "You were right about it being different when I take you with making a baby in mind."

I giggled and slipped my arms around his waist, snuggling against his chest. "It sure is."

Two weeks later, a positive pregnancy test confirmed we were successful in our mission. And nine months after that, we had another baby boy who looked just like his father.

Curious about Nic DeLuca and his wife? Find out how they got together in The Mafia Boss's Nanny!

And if you join our newsletter, you'll get an email from us with a link to claim a FREE copy of The Virgin's Guardian, which was banned on Amazon.

ABOUT THE AUTHOR

The writing duo of Elle Christensen and Rochelle Paige team up under the Fiona Davenport pen name to bring you sexy, insta-love stories filled with alpha males. If you want a quick & dirty read with a guaranteed happily ever after, then give Fiona Davenport a try!

Printed in Great Britain
by Amazon